GROWING PAINS

A Teenager's War

Wish Best Wishes
Gwendoline Page

GROWING PAINS

A Teenager's War

Gwendoline Page

The Book Guild Ltd.
Sussex, England

The Book Guild Ltd.
25 High Street,
Lewes, Sussex

First published 1994
© Gwendoline Page 1994
Set in Baskerville
Typesetting by Raven Typesetters
Ellesmere Port, South Wirral
Printed in Great Britain by
Antony Rowe Ltd.
Chippenham, Wiltshire.

A catalogue record for this book
is available from the British Library

ISBN 0 86332 910 1

Acknowledgements

I should like to acknowledge the following authors and their books for jogging my memory and spurring me to put pen to paper.

The Forties by Alan Jenkins.
Keep Smiling Through by Susan Briggs.
War Isn't Wonderful by Ursula Bloom.
Ultra Goes to War by Ronald Lewin,
Convoy by Martin Middlebrook.
An article in *Saga* by William Foster.
The Fringes of Power by John Colville.
Road to Victory by Martin Gilbert.
P.R. Melton of the Naval Historical Library.
Bridget Spiers of Ministry of Defence Whitehall Library.
John Burton of Swaffham for information concerning evacuees.
Rev. Arthur Royall for his memories of Arnhem.
Also many others who helped me with their own recollections.

My grateful thanks also to my daughter Fiona who typed out the manuscript for me numerous times due to inserts and alterations and who now probably knows it all by heart!

I must not forget to give my sincere appreciation and multi thanks to my husband Harry for taking on many household tasks and allowing me to spend more time on the writing of this book, while he kept the home running on 'an even keel'.

G.M. Page

Introduction

In the great surge of nostalgia recalling the years between 1939–45 I noticed that among all the war stories and picture books of the period I could see nothing written by someone whose whole teenage life was taken up by those years.

In talking with my daughters and other members of a younger generation, I found the differences in life and style of living so vast as to be almost unbelievable by some youngsters. It was on my daughters' and son-in-laws' suggestion that I started to write of the way we faced growing up in a country at war; the things we did; the things we did without; the changes that were made; the everyday incidents and the spells of excitement or fear.

For most civilians these years were a seemingly never-ending period of fear, frustration and hardship, particularly so for those facing long separations from husbands, sons or daughters serving in danger areas on land, at sea or in the air, in Britain and abroad. Even those who lived or retreated to the depths of the country away from the bombing were often unwilling guests of reluctant hosts, separated from family and friends in a strange environment. Others found kindness, affection and love, many of them to settle and live permanently in their adopted towns and villages.

Excitement came to a fewer number of people, but excitement of the pleasurable kind was more rare. Our country, our homes, our very lives were at stake and in this story I try to tell how a generation coped with the problems of living, loving and possibly dying, whilst yet still finding something to laugh about in a time of devastation and uncertainty. Not all of us were heroes or heroines, simply ordinary young people trying to do

7

the best we could in a world which seemed hell-bent on annihilation. In the process many discovered unsuspected strengths and weaknesses within themselves.

The war caused changes of attitudes, breaking down many of the rigid class barriers and set rules of behaviour which had been in force up until that time, engendering a better appreciation of one another's qualities and a sense of neighbourliness which had not always been apparent before. Perhaps it was the beginning of the breakdown of our so-called British reserve, helped by the overwhelming great goodheartedness we received from complete strangers in our own land, our dominions and from the people of the United States of America and others overseas. Some links have been dissolved by time, but many still survive and will be continued by our children and hopefully our grandchildren, though we pray that they may never have to experience the same testing period of war.

I was one of the lucky ones. My story covers part of the 1930s in peace time, through the outbreak of war in 1939 until the end of 1945 when I was twenty years of age. From school days; family life; rationing and the Blitz; the impact of foreign service personnel; to service in Britain and the Far East with the Women's Royal Naval Service and the end of war.

1

A Teenager's War

Well . . . that title is not strictly true as in the years of 1939 to
1945 the word 'teenager' had not been heard of in Britain. The
term 'teenager' came many years later, brought to these shores
by our trans-Atlantic cousins. Up until then young people
between the ages of thirteen and nineteen were simply
children, youth, kids or even brats. In one of her films, Judy
Garland sang a song in which she said she was 'too old for toys
and too young for boys, I'm just an in between', which I
thought put our situation very neatly. Newspaper reports
described anyone under the age of twenty-one as 'a minor'.
After twenty-one, with the 'key of the door' came your
majority, the vote and adulthood.

In 1939 I was living with my parents, brother and sister in a
pleasant detached house, down a quiet road, in a small village,
in the county of Hertfordshire, about thirteen miles outside
the London boundary. My parents were comparatively well
off, owning their own small business, a newsagent's, tobac-
conist's and sweet shop. The shop also included a toy and fancy
goods' section and a lending library which gave the shop its
name, 'The Library', written in curvy flowing letters on a
signboard above the double-fronted windows. The business
was run jointly by my parents with the aid of a full time
manager and several lady assistants who had all been with my
parents for many years.

To help in the home we had a maid, Catherine, who lived in
rooms over the shop which was only five minutes' walk from
our house. Catherine had come to us in the years of the big

depression, during the early 1930s. Her home was in Durham in the north of England and we children were intrigued by her strange speech and regional accent, but in time we grew to understand and like her. It is difficult for a child to judge age, but I think she must have been in her twenties when she was with us. I remember her as fair and slim and although we must have plagued her at times, I do not remember her becoming bad tempered. In fact I believe we all got along quite nicely and my parents valued her highly enough to leave her in charge of the house and us when they took a rare holiday to Jersey or Ireland.

My brother and I had both attended a small private school in the area until the age of nine when we passed an entrance exam to become fee paying pupils at the old grammar school, established in 1578, according to the date carved on a gatepost, in the reign of the first Queen Elizabeth in the nearby town of Barnet. Boys' and girls' schools were in separate newer buildings in different parts of town; the girls' school dating from 1887, but on the same bus route and within fifteen minutes walking distance of each other. As I was two years older than my brother, I was already well settled in school by the time he started there.

Our sister, six years younger than myself was considered by us as still a baby. She was also considered a bit of a nuisance at times, especially when we were both engrossed in reading some exciting story or other activity which was interrupted by her wishing to leave the room for some reason, the problem being that all door handles were too high for her to reach. This meant that one of us had to get up in order to open the door. Neither of us hurried to oblige, but each sat there waiting for the other to move while our sister's requests became more demanding and noisy. Eventually one would give way and reluctantly rise from the chair or rug on which we sat and go to let her out. We would then return to our book and become involved in the story once more only to be interrupted a few minutes later by Cindy knocking on the door wanting to come back in again.

The three of us suffered from the usual childish ailments of those days; measles, German measles, whooping cough, mumps and chickenpox, but we managed to avoid the scourge of Scarlet fever. Scarlet fever was a common disease, much more serious than the former mentioned measles etc. which could be treated at home. I remember seeing an ambulance arrive at my friend's home one day and watching from my window as the men brought her out of the house on a stretcher. She was wrapped in a thick red blanket and lying very still as they put her in to the back of the ambulance. The doors were shut and the ambulance drove off. I asked my mother, 'Where are they taking her?' 'To the isolation hospital,' was her reply. For some reason, it was the sight of the bright red blanket which disturbed me more than anything. I was five years old at the time. Perhaps my parents had impressed my young mind with the fact that the colour red was used for indicating danger. Certainly, that red blanket caused me to feel scared for my friend, and my mind was not entirely at rest until she was safely home again.

Grazed and cut knees, elbows and other areas of limbs were treated with iodine and improvised bandages, often made from strips of old torn sheeting. We disliked the iodine which stung when it was applied and caused us to screw up our faces to try to be brave and avoid the shame of tears. Such convenient remedies as sticking plaster I cannot remember seeing until some time later during the war years. I do remember the problem we had with bandages, especially those put around the knees. It seemed that either the bandage was pulled so tight that it made my leg too stiff, preventing me from running as fast as my friends, or it became loose and dangled down my leg, causing constant halts in my play in order to adjust it. As all small boys wore short trousers in the 1930s there were many young warriors sporting a bandaged knee. Other more indefinable pains in legs or arms were always referred to as 'growing pains'. They have been with me all my life and as I grow older the 'pains' grow more. But I don't think that was quite what Mother meant!

On weekends when the weather was fine, my parents often took us out for a drive in their Standard Eight car. Sometimes we went to a beautiful woodland area where in the Spring,

ROLLING ORANGES ON DUNSTABLE DOWNS

bluebells formed a hazy carpet of blue around us, or to other places where primroses grew in an abundance of yellow clusters on grassy banks. Our parents enjoyed the quiet beauty of such places after the cares and busy week of the business and we younger members of the family revelled in the freedom to run, play hide and seek and climb trees in the glorious sunshine of youth. Other visits were made to the Dunstable Downs to watch the gliders take off from the sides of the downs and gradually ascend in the thermal currents to circle around above our heads like great silent birds. As far as I can remember the gliders were launched by manpower in those days. Certainly there were no aeroplanes towing them off the ground. I believe teams of men on ropes stretched down the hillside somehow catapulted the gliders into the air. It must have been a hazardous sport then. Later, cars were used to tow the gliders.

One Easter Sunday or Monday, my brother, sister and I joined hundreds of other children on the slopes of the Downs to scramble for the oranges the adults rolled down to us, a custom which probably had its origins in egg rolling. It looked easy from above, but it was quite a feat to grab the rolling orange balls without losing one's footing and rolling down the hill along with the oranges. However, we all managed at least one. orange and so were satisfied with our efforts.

Some weekends we were taken to visit my mother's mother in Surrey. Granny lived in a Victorian detached house which had a very large cypress tree in the front garden which obscured most of the view from the front window. Since the front room or parlour was only used on Sundays or special occasions it appeared not to worry Granny that she was unable to see much of the passers-by. Granny was small, short-sighted and always wore a long black dress occasionally relieved by a touch of white, or a black and white sprigged apron. Her grey hair was coiled into a bun at the nape of her neck and rested on her high frilled collar. She took little notice of her grandchildren, having had quite enough of her own children, some of whom still lived close by. This was the only time we met up with some of our cousins as they rarely travelled our way. At these times pranks occurred and as all our cousins were male I had to be especially wary of such things as apple-pie beds and other jokes of which I was frequently the recipient, but usually managed to repay these attentions in kind.

As a young child, I remember Granny sewing in the light of a softly glowing oil lamp which stood tall and shiny in the middle of the dining-table, her grey head bent close to her work. The warm smell of the lamp only added to the sense of cosiness. The main part of the house was lit by gas. Its flickering light cast dancing shadows on the walls of my bedroom and the soft hissing and popping sounds emitted from the delicate filament within the white glass globe gave reign to my vivid imagination as I lay in the big brass bed. When the pictures in my mind became too scary, I snuggled deeper under the covers and pulled the big feather eiderdown over my head. Granny fought valiantly against the age of electricity, but eventually her daughters overcame her scruples and electric light and power were installed throughout the house.

Visits to our other grandparents' house were more formal and adult as there were no other grandchildren on my father's side of the family. Grandpa had been a well-established member of the Yorkshire Insurance Company and had retired on an excellent pension for those times. His large house and garden, maintained with the help of maid and gardener, was slightly overwhelming to our young spirits, although he, a quiet and gentle man, was never repressive. He rarely joined in our games, but was a willing tutor when it came to bee keeping and the making of honey, a long-time hobby of his. Arrayed in wide-brimmed straw hats with long veils and thick gloves we were allowed to watch while he puffed clouds of smoke over the open hives to calm the bees before removing the frames coated in wax and glistening honey. Sometimes Alan or I were allowed the great pleasure of working the puff gun.

Aunt Helen, my father's step-mother who had no children of her own, saw that we were kept busy and amused, joining in the activities where she had time. We were both very fond of her, but were a little shy of showing our feelings.

At the age of nine or thereabouts I was given a bicycle. Green in colour, it was the apple of my eye and gave me great pleasure for two or three years until I outgrew it. At twelve years of age my green bicycle was put on one side to await my sister while I graduated to a larger black cycle. In the years before the war, traffic consisted of horses and carts, some vans and lorries for commercial purposes, but few cars.

The Dutch Oven Bakery which stood at the corner of the main street and the road in which we lived, where the aroma of freshly baked bread tickled the nose and appetite of every passer-by, used beautiful cart-horses to pull their delivery vans. The baker's son bore the imprint of one of the horse's hooves on his face, which had been a little too close when the horse kicked out. Our milk was also delivered by horse and cart, the milkman's horse knowing exactly when to move and stop outside each house without instructions from the milkman. Where the horses stood for a while, they frequently left a small reminder of their presence. I well remember my mother giving me a bucket and shovel and telling me to collect this 'for the roses' in the days before garden manure arrived neatly packaged in plastic bags. Some cars were owned by the better off members of the population, but most people owned bicycles, walked or used buses to attend their daily work. In general people did not travel any long distance to their jobs but lived close to where their work was situated. We as children were free to cycle anywhere around our village and the neighbouring countryside without fear or worry, on our parents' part, as long as we were back in good time for our meals. This enabled us to explore our environment at will and we grew knowing where every lane and path led, enjoying the delights of fields and woodlands, ponds and streams and of the plants, animals, birds and aquatic creatures dwelling within them. Life for us children was sunny, settled and secure.

My parents were members of the Baptist Church and as children we attended chapel most Sundays for morning service, although as my sister was still so young we children were excused the sermon and second part of the service. It was my responsibility to take Alan and Cindy home while my parents stayed on. I was extremely glad to escape so easily as the minister, a charming though shy man, was apt to get carried away with his fervour and preach for an hour or more in his zeal, with threats of hell and damnation for the wicked, and many a Sunday dinner was spoilt. There seemed to be so many taboos on pleasures I enjoyed like dancing and certain games that could not be played, especially on a Sunday, that I am afraid I was a somewhat rebellious member of his flock.

There were no other girls of my age living in our road, consequently my playmates were the half dozen or so boys who resided there. As a result of this I became a regular tomboy who could climb trees, wrestle, play cricket or football with the best of them and was accepted as an equal by the group. The difference in sex was not regarded by my friends as being of any importance; what was important was the fact that I could bowl straight and catch a hard ball. When a visiting group of boys wanted to play a game of cricket against my friends, but scorned and rejected a girl playing with them, my loyal pals refused to join them unless I was also given a place in the team. The visitors reluctantly agreed. I repaid their magnanimity by bowling out their captain first ball! Strangely, after this I was accepted without any further protests or remarks.

Although a fairly well-developed young girl in all the usual places, it was not until I was fourteen that my sex aroused other attitudes. My mother had taken my brother, sister, myself and another girlfriend on holiday to Great Yarmouth. It was a sunny summer in 1939 and we spent most of our time on the beach in our swimsuits. I was running back from the water to my family when a boy whistled a wolf call to me and said, 'Hello mermaid'. I was astonished at his behaviour and after one startled look ignored him and continued on my way. This event did not alter my attitude to my long-standing friends at home and theirs remained the same to me for another year or so, but it gave me cause to ponder why I should have been awarded such attention and from then on I was rather wary of young male strangers.

Such a reaction on my part must seem surprising and almost unbelievable to present day young people who have a much more casual and open approach to one another. But relationships in general were much more formal in the 1930s when few people addressed one another by their first name apart from members of the family. Although we had the same neighbours for twenty years and were on friendly terms, my mother and our neighbour invariably addressed one another by surname, always Mrs A . . . or Mrs J. . . . Never did I hear them use Christian names. Even my mother's closest friends whose houses we visited reasonably often and who in turn visited us, were always Mrs C . . . and Mrs D . . . when addressed.

My upbringing was in a strict nonconformist, teetotal background. My parents were not inclined towards social occasions. One reason was that the business gave them little time to do so and a second reason was, I believe, that they were both basically shy. My father was a gentle, quiet man, an observer rather than a partaker of life. Mother was the more dominant character of the two in house and business, but she came from an even stricter nonconformist background where dancing, theatre-going and other such joys were highly suspect and the only leisure activities permitted on a Sunday were church, reading the Bible or going for a walk with the family. For this reason I believe she lacked confidence when it came to socialising out of the family circle.

As children we were informed that it was incorrect to speak to someone unless you had first been introduced to them, therefore our circle of friends was strictly limited. The war changed people's attitudes; formality relaxed in times of trouble, never quite returning to these set and rigid rules of behaviour.

The pattern of life continued as usual for myself and my family and friends at school, with visits to relatives and the annual seaside holiday as the focal points and highlights of the year.

A wave of interest was caused at school when a new pupil joined our class unexpectedly in the middle of the term. Most pupils joined at the beginning of term and there were few changes. My classmates and I had been through the school together since we joined at the age of nine, apart from three or four friends who came to join us at the age of eleven through

17

scholarships from the elementary state schools of the surrounding area. This girl was different, she was German and spoke halting English with an attractive accent. Apart from one other girl who was Spanish and had come to England at the time of the Spanish Civil War, we had no other girls of foreign nationality in our school and met very few in our town or villages. Rita was quiet, shy but pleasant and for a while was the centre of attention, probably much to her embarrassment. She was immediately accepted by the class and requested by some to help in checking over their German homework for them before it was handed in for the scrutiny of the teacher. She spoke little of her home in Germany or why she was in England. At that time we knew nothing of the unrest going on in Germany and of the dreadful treatment of the Jewish people there. It was only much later that I connected this knowledge with Rita's arrival.

It was not until 1938 that rumours of possible war began to invade the conversations of the adults around us. In September 1938 the fleet was called up. I noticed that my parents' faces became anxious and their voices low and serious in tone when discussing the rumours with other adults. My mother thought it might be wise to start stocking up the cupboards and larder with extra tins of various foods in case of an emergency or shortage of supplies. There was talk of air-raids and gas-masks. People recounted stories of Zeppelin raids in the Great War of 1914–1918 only twenty years previously and still a recent memory for so many. Old soldiers remembered their experiences of battle and life in the trenches and looked grave. The undercurrent of apprehension flowed through our village contaminating all, but whereas our parents and their contemporaries felt unease and fear, we youngsters, without that knowledge, felt only excitement.

Then Neville Chamberlain, the Prime Minister, went to Munich to meet Hitler, the German leader who was the cause of all this alarm. Chamberlain came back waving his piece of paper and saying we would have 'peace in our time'. Everyone heaved a sigh of relief and went back to work. Mother stopped worrying about food shortages, the price of eggs remained the same as they had done for the last five years or more, faces became brighter with smiles and laughter and all reverted to normal.

2

Peace continued for us in Britain throughout Winter and Spring and into Summer, then once again concern darkened countenances as men and women gathered around the wireless sets for the news broadcasts and we children were forbidden to speak or make any sound while the newscaster read his script. The name 'Poland' occurred often. Apart from realising that it was a country situated somewhere in the middle of Europe, most people knew little about it, but in the summer of 1939 Poland became the crux of Britain's decision for peace or war.

We had only recently returned from our holiday in Great Yarmouth and a school friend and I had been out for a cycle ride, enjoying the last few days before the start of the new school term. It was 3 September 1939. Joyce and I came back to my home to find my parents around the wireless set on which it had just been announced that the prime minister was to speak. My brother and sister were already there and we all waited quietly to hear what he had to say. The quiet, gentle voice of Neville Chamberlain flowed through the room and with evident sadness informed us that Hitler's troops had invaded Poland and that consequently we were now at war with Germany!

Now that it had actually happened, war definitely declared, we youngsters were filled with a subdued excitement, but my father who had been through the First World War and only missed the carnage of the Dardenells by a lucky appendix which necessitated removing him from the battle zone to the safety of a hospital in Egypt, shook his head sadly. His memories were too near to cause any other reactions but apprehension and despondency.

In the previous few weeks there had been much talk and many articles printed about the things that must be done should such an emergency occur, and my practical mother immediately set her mind to work on these subjects. The glass windows must be criss-crossed with sticky brown paper to prevent shattering from blast, blackout curtains must be made and hung at all windows to prevent light shining through, food must be considered and restocked and numerous other details attended to. In the rush to comply with these regulations, shops ran out of blackout material, drawing-pins and tin-tacks.

My father was trying to cope with the questions my brother and I were flinging at him in the excitement of the moments following the announcement, 'What will happen now?' 'Will we be bombed?' 'Will we still go to school?', when suddenly the air-raid sirens began to wail. This startled us into silence as we heard the rise and fall of their continual eerie warning which must have penetrated the deafest of ears.

'Quick' said Mother, 'gather all the cushions and pile them on top of the table and then get underneath it.'

This we did. Crouching under this crude form of shelter we listened for the sound of aircraft and falling bombs which we expected to hear, but there was nothing. Much to my parents' great relief, after a while the sustained note of the all-clear signal sounded out. Crawling out from between the legs of the table and replacing the cushions seemed a bit of an anti-climax and rather ridiculous. Later we heard that there had been no raid, but it was a practice alert to see how people and defence services reacted. Although we had not suffered in this first alert, we had news a few days later that the liner *Athenia* had been sunk by a U-boat on 3 or 4 September, the first casualty after the declaration of war.

For some time life appeared to continue close to normal for the younger members of the community. Apart from the appearance of blackout curtains and sticky tape on the windows of shops and houses, and the gigantic air-raid siren which stood on a corner beside the blue and white police box, our village looked much as usual. But changes were taking place in the adult world. Young men disappeared from village life to reappear in smart new uniforms of khaki, navy or air force blue. Those unable to join the regular services played their part by volunteering for the Local Defence Force, called the Local Defence Volunteers or LDV, self-deprecatingly called by some of its members the 'Look, Duck and Vanish Corps'. They were later renamed the Home Guard. To begin with their only uniform was an armband bearing the letters LDV and possibly a tin helmet. Eventually all were provided with khaki battledress, greatcoat, forage caps and shoulder flashes denoting their membership of the Home Guard, very similar to the uniform of the regular army. Others became air raid wardens, fire-watchers, members of the Observer Corps spotting lone enemy raiders and other offensive aircraft in order to pass on warnings, special constables attached to the police force, or joined the fire service.

Unprepared as we had been for war, weapons were so scarce that even the Territorial Army did not have sufficient rifles; certainly there was no surplus with which to arm the Local Defence Force. Instead of rifles, there was talk of arming them with pikes, long handled spears similar to those carried by the Yeomen at The Tower of London. The Local Defence Volunteers certainly practised with dummy rifles for some time until the country was in a position to give them a reasonable supply of real ones.

The manager of my father's shop was one of the first of the faces we missed and so my parents became involved with the daily work of running the business, although a reliable young lady was promoted as an assistant manager. Catherine decided to return home to Durham to be near her family. We were sorry to see her go. Mother managed to find other help by getting a lady from the village to come in to do housework two mornings a week, but of course much of the household duties and all the cooking she now had to do herself. Alan and I were also given various tasks and had to take our turn with the washing-up. I was taught to cook the Sunday lunch, make pastry, rice pudding and a few other simple dishes.

Ration books were issued and on 8 January 1940 food rationing commenced. Each book had to be marked with its

What do they have today?

owner's name, address and national registration number, for example, BCCE 89 3. Under headings of MILK, MEAT, EGGS, FAT, CHEESE, BACON, SUGAR, there had to be a rubber stamp mark bearing the name of the retailer with whom you shopped. Then under the same food headings were pages marked out in weeks and as each week's ration was bought, that week was marked off by the retailer. Coupons for other items consumed, e.g. sweets, were cut out from the book separately. At the beginning of the war there was still plenty of food to be had, but further imports had to be cut to allow shipping space to be used for materials and implements of war instead. All cinemas, theatres, dance halls and even football matches which caused people to congregate in large numbers were barred for fear of bombing, although church services continued as usual. The BBC was left with a monopoly on entertainment. This closure ban did not last long. Entertainment was discovered to be a great morale booster and people were willing to take a chance on the bombs.

Householders were asked to dig up their lawns and plant vegetables in their place. 'Dig for Victory' posters were seen on every hoarding. Those with enough room and inclination took to keeping a pig to provide a juicy joint or two. My father decided to turn the end of our garden into a chicken run. It was my duty to feed them and Alan's duty to muck out, or clean the hen house every week. Mother stored some of the resulting eggs in a large bucket in isinglass solution to be used in the off-lay period. We kept a cockerel of which I was a little afraid, but I loved the little fluffy yellow chicks which were the outcome of his attention to the hens. When a hen went broody she was put into a separate little coop to sit on her eggs. The hatching of these eggs was a fascinating delight to us youngsters. To watch the shells breaking, see the tiny damp chicks tumble out and within a short space of time become a scampering yellow ball on matchstick legs was to us one of nature's marvels.

Another new feature to grace our garden was a large grassy mound upon that which had been flat lawn. This was the Anderson air-raid shelter, named after the chief of air-raid precautions, Sir John Anderson. The basic shelter was delivered to each home as sheets of curved corrugated iron with accompanying nuts and bolts. It was then up to the house-holders to erect it for themselves. It took my father some hard digging to make a pit about three feet deep and six feet by four feet in size in solid clay soil and then to dig a further smaller, deeper pit to act as a sump in order to drain the water which accumulated on the clay base. He then had to erect the corrugated metal pieces and bolt them together in the form of an arch. This was accomplished with help from the family who were required to help attach the end pieces, then strengthen their muscles by shovelling all the soil removed from the pit and pile it around and on top of the iron to add further protection to the shelter. The final touches to the outside were grass turfs cut from the lawn and laid over the whole erection to keep the soil in place. Steps had been cut in the ground to allow access to the small entrance into which a slotted door was fitted. Inside Dad had made a wooden platform above the clay floor on which to stand, also three wooden bunks for us to sleep on. Further refinements were a small wooden table and a paraffin lamp which hung from a bolt in the roof. In this cave-like dwelling we were to spend many damp, disturbed nights.

Those families without gardens were issued with another form of shelter called the 'Morrison', named after Herbert Morrison, a cabinet minister for the Home Office at the time, which was introduced in 1941. The 'Morrison' was a large flat-topped table-height structure, reinforced with wire mesh and cement which was placed in one of the main rooms. It was supposed to replace the use of a conventional table, but its main purpose was to provide protection for as many as could crouch or lie beneath its solid surface.

Other monstrosities to appear were the hideous gas-masks. If one suffered from even the slightest form of claustrophobia, these ugly appendices were agony to wear. Notices were posted telling people when and where to report, usually in alpha-betical order at the local church hall, and there men and women of the local ARP (Air-Raid Precaution) group issued the masks and gave instruction on how to use them. I still remember with distaste the smell of the rubber that clamped around your face, the pull of the webbing on your head, the way the small celluloid window clouded over with your breath and the constricted breathing it engendered. One was told to breathe easily and steadily to enable the mask to work correctly, not an easy thing to do at the height of a crisis. Special Mickey Mouse masks were provided for some of the younger children and other forms of masks for babies in arms. Luckily no occasion ever arose when we were required to wear them, although it was obligatory to carry them in a box case suspended from a shoulder strap, wherever you went. Also obligatory were the identity cards which had your photograph, name and address printed on them. These had to be produced on demand by police or guards of the armed forces; to acquire new ration books, clothing coupons and for a hundred and one other reasons. If you had no identity card you were a non-entity, you just didn't exist or, worse, you were an enemy, a spy or something similar.

To the adults in our lives all these new restrictions were irritating and tedious, but generally borne with resignation. We younger members accepted them as they came as part of the order of life and left our parents to worry and cope. We continued with school, homework and meeting our friends for play much as normal. Joyce and I cycled the five miles to school and five miles home without fear or interruption throughout the period of the so called phoney war which lasted well into 1940. Our parents and teachers had told us that should an air-raid take place on our way to school or home, we were to knock on the door of a nearby house and ask for shelter. We felt this could be quite an adventure, and looked forward to a chance to be invited into one of the large and imposing looking properties set back from the common through which we cycled every week day. However, to our disappointment the opportunity never occurred.

During this time we experienced little hostile activity apart from one or two alerts from the sirens to keep us on our toes, but preparations were going ahead and we were given talks by Civil Defence personnel in what to do in case of raids, how to deal with fire-bombs with the aid of sandbags, buckets of sand or water. My recollection of these buckets of sand positioned in strategic points in corridors and passages is that they were mostly used as convenient ashtrays and were studded with cigarette ends. Dad bought a stirrup pump and gave us lessons on how to use it by putting one end of the hose in a bucket of water, holding the base of the pump on the ground with our feet and pumping the horizontal handle steadily up and down until the water spurted out of the other end of the hose. Two persons were required to work it successfully. We never had need to use it against incendiary bombs or fire, but it gave us much pleasure in the hot summers of these years as a method of cooling off.

In the summer of 1940 instead of the long holiday, the school remained open for pupils to participate in pleasurable activities such as tennis and other games, music and art; a school for recreation in fact. Most teachers took advantage of the good weather, holding classes out of doors in the pleasant school grounds. The freedom of the art classes where we were encouraged to sketch and paint the nearby landscape, and the relaxed attitudes of our teachers, made it a very enjoyable experience. For the first time formality was discarded and we felt able to chat or discuss our ambitions, hopes and fears with our teachers as with any adult friend.

Alan spent his summer holiday, along with others from his school on a farm, helping the farmer to get in the harvest. He came home at the end of the holiday somewhat leaner than he went, with the knees out of his trousers from stooking sheaves of corn, standing the cut and bound sheaves upright, one against another to dry out in the summer sun and breezes: a field of golden wigwams. No combine harvesters then, it was hard manual work. My mother was most upset, but I am not sure which upset her more, the fact of Alan's loss of weight or the thought of the difficulty in providing new trousers.

On the outbreak of war many children from the cities were evacuated to country areas through a government sponsored scheme. A number of their teachers went with them. One group of around fourteen hundred children, mothers and some teachers from Dagenham in Essex and Gravesend in Kent were

27

evacuated and taken by sea around the East coast of England to Great Yarmouth in Norfolk. They were then transported in a fleet of thirty-one double-decker buses to East Dereham in Norfolk. The billeting officer and his staff of six assistants had been recalled to work the day before, the day war was declared, Sunday, 3 September, to be ready to receive this great influx of extra people on the Monday.

Some preparations had been made in case such an emergency should occur and a list of those willing to house evacuees was ready. Dereham, however, was not a very large town and the list of willing hosts was soon exhausted. It was then up to the billeting officers to persuade the unwilling and reluctant householders with room available to change their minds. The young and attractive lady billeting officers had more success in this direction than their male counterparts. Where charm and persuasion failed, billeting officers had to use their powers of enforcement under the Emergency Powers Act. This all took a great deal of time. It was late at night before all evacuees were finally housed.

On the Tuesday morning the billeting officer returned to his office to find a long queue of evacuee mothers and children awaiting him. They had come to complain. In colourful language containing numerous adjectives they expressed their dissatisfaction with their accommodation and the area in general and said they wanted to go home! During the first week fifty per cent did so. After three weeks only two hundred and fifty of the original fourteen hundred remained. After three months only one hundred were still in Dereham.

At outbreak of war people had been scared that towns would be immediately subjected to bombing and gas attacks. This did not materialise, so a false sense of security prevailed. With the approach of Christmas some suffered a sense of homesickness and wanted to be in their own home for the celebrations. Others missed the facilities of a large town and did not take kindly to the countryside. Another reason may have been the fact that there were a number of airfields in the vicinity and they were just as likely to be the target of bombing raids as were Dagenham or Gravesend. If they had the choice of where they were going to be bombed it might as well be at home!

The local council authorities such as the billeting officers had spent many hours finding accommodation and issuing billeting tickets of eight shillings and sixpence for each adult and five shillings for each child to be given to the host for payment. Dereham Food Office also was required to provide ration cards for the whole fourteen hundred. Apart from this it was necessary to liaise with the social services and hospitals for the care of forty-seven of the women who were expectant mothers. Then within four months most of this great invasion of human population had returned from whence they came, leaving only a remnant of less than one hundred in this small East Anglian town. Although it may not have been a success in terms of resettlement of citizens from danger areas as the Government had hoped, it was no doubt a useful lesson on problems to be encountered in any future emergencies.

Other families sent their children abroad to relatives, friends and hosts in Canada, USA and other areas well away from the conflict of Europe. There was much discussion between my mother and father as to whether we three children should also be evacuated and Alan and I were asked if we would be willing to go. My father had already contacted a relative in South Africa who was willing to take us. To me, at fourteen years of age, the prospect of travelling and a chance to see a foreign country was exciting and adventurous. So far all my travels and explorations had been made through the black and white and just occasionally colourful pages of a book. Alan, then twelve years old, was also willing to make the move. He had, at the age of seven, decided he wanted to be a sailor and the vision of a long sea voyage took his fancy. Neither of us seemed to be worried about a possible long-term separation from our parents. Of course we had no knowledge that the war was to last for six years. Mother decided that Cindy was too young to go with us and she would stay at home, but plans and arrangements went ahead for Alan and I. Medical examinations were made at our respective schools and all the necessary forms filled in. Suitable clothes were sorted out and

29

we tried to read all we could about our expected destination.

Then disaster struck! On 17 September 1940 the *City of Benares*, a ship carrying hundreds of children being evacuated to North America was torpedoed by a U-boat, a German submarine, in the North Atlantic Sea and ninety-three children were lost. The shock reverberated throughout the country and many parents withdrew their consent to any further evacuations, my parents amongst them. Alan and I were at first disappointed that our travelling was curtailed, but so many new things were happening that we soon adjusted to the situation.

In the quiet period before the Blitz of 1940, many of those other families evacuated to the countryside earlier were lulled into a false sense of security and returned to London. News from our forces on the continent was not good. My parents, faces became more and more concerned as Hitler continued his invasion of neutral countries. Norway, Denmark, Holland and Belgium and into France. No one seemed able to stop him. Whenever my father was home the radio was on and every time there was a news flash the whole family became silent. Even Alan and I were now aware of the seriousness of the situation.

The poorly equipped Allied forces in France, their movements hampered by the great mass of refugees fleeing before the German army, were unable to prevent Hitler's tanks breaking through and in June 1940 were ordered to retreat to Dunkirk where those who were not killed or captured were evacuated by the Royal Navy helped by a flotilla of small boats manned by fishermen and part-time sailors. Anyone who had a small craft at his or her disposal set out across the Channel to bring home as many of the Allied soldiers as possible. In doing so they suffered bombing and strafing attacks by enemy aircraft and some never made the return journey. Those who did went time and time again to bring back our men until it was no longer feasible to do so. The official title for this evacuation was 'Operation Dynamo'.

Some of my cousins who were in the Territorial Army when war broke out and were sent to France with the British Expeditionary Forces were among the lucky ones brought

30

home by such means. One told us he had actually been captured by German soldiers, but had been deliberately allowed to escape by the young private set to guard him. Jumping into a ditch he made his way to the beach by working along the hedgerows, endeavouring to stay out of sight of the numerous German patrols. Another, a dispatch rider who found himself without transport and had visions of a long walk to the coast, found a horse and tried to ride him, but was not too successful in communicating his wishes to the animal. Every man on finding himself cut off from his unit took whatever means he could to reach the coast.

On 8 June 1940 the remaining British troops of those sent to Narvik in April, were also evacuated from Norway. On 11 June Italy declared war on Great Britain. On 22 June France capitulated and a few days later German troops moved into Britain's Channel Islands. People's morale was at a low ebb at this point, but I never heard any talk of surrender. Churchill was now prime minister and rallied the country with his fine speeches. On 4 June he spoke these words in the House of Commons:

'Even though large tracts of Europe have fallen into the grip of the Gestapo, and all the odious apparatus of Nazi rule, we shall not flag or fail, we shall go on to the end. We shall fight in France. We shall fight on the seas and oceans. We shall fight with growing confidence and growing strength in the air. We shall defend our Island, whatever the cost may be. We shall fight on the beaches. We shall fight on the landing grounds. We shall fight in the fields and streets. We shall fight in the hills. We shall never surrender. And even if, which I do not for a moment believe, this Island or a large part of it were subjugated and starving, then our Empire beyond the oceans armed and guarded by the British fleet, will carry on the struggle until in God's good time the New World with all its power and might sets forth to the rescue and liberation of the old.'

All took new heart and a determination not to give up.

Our next door neighbour received a shock one morning on answering a knock at her door. On her doorstep stood her cousin with her nineteen year old daughter, suitcases in hand. They had made a hurried flight from Jersey on one of the last ships to leave before the island was occupied by German forces. Her cousin's husband had stayed behind to guard his home as well as he could. They had nothing apart from what they carried. Our neighbour took them in and there they stayed for several years not knowing what was happening to husband and home in the Channel Islands.

Once Hitler had command of the Channel ports, the air-raids became more frequent and more intense. The threat of invasion was in everyone's mind. At school our lessons were frequently interrupted by an air-raid warning when we immediately stopped whatever we were doing, picked up our gas-masks and were ushered out of the classroom to safer parts of the building. At this time the school had no specially built shelters, so we went to small windowless passages or under stone stairways where we sat on the floor resting our backs against the walls while our teachers hovered at the entrance of the passages to keep an eye on us and remain alert to the raid. Sometimes the raiders passed over quickly on their way to other targets and our town was unmolested. Then we returned to our lessons at the sound of the all-clear to continue our work until the next alert. At other times the raids were longer and more severe and we whiled away the time playing simple games such as 'I spy', chatting or singing. I had always been a keen singer of all kinds of music and had memorised many folk songs, old ballads, popular songs from the radio, musical shows, operettas and films, the young film star singer Deanna Durbin being a great favourite of mine at the time. So while the bombers droned overhead I sang to take our minds off what was happening outside. Since my captive audience never threw anything at me or asked me to stop, I assumed they enjoyed it or at least did not mind too much. Certainly I had requests from both my class mates and the staff to write out the words of some of the songs for them.

Barnet, the town in which I went to school, was situated just outside the protective ring of barrage balloons encircling London. These huge, silver monsters, tethered to earth by strong metal cables, floated high in the sky on the outskirts of the city and were attended by teams of army and ATS (Auxiliary Territorial Service) personnel, one of the more physically active forms of war work in which the women were allowed to participate. Their purpose was to deflect the enemy bombers from their bombing run into the city and cause them to have to fly much higher in order to drop their bombs on target. Our fighter crews endeavoured to attack the enemy planes outside the barrage and turn them from their course, destroying as many as possible in the process. Enemy fighters sometimes machine-gunned the balloons which caught fire, dropping to earth in a flare of orange flame.

Frequently raiders unable to get through this defence dropped their bombs wherever they were in order to lighten their load to return to base. Consequently small towns and villages like ours were often the recipients of these unwelcome gifts. So it was that as we sat chatting or singing in our improvised shelter we recognised the drone of an enemy bomber, the whistle of its deadly load as it came screaming down to earth, then the 'Krrump' of contact which sent vibrations through the walls and floors and made the lamps swing and windows rattle. Surrounded as we were by many fields and open spaces, it was only an unlucky few who caught the full impact of a bomb on their building and I do not remember an actual human fatality in our village although there were some near misses and some bizarre sights. Our coalman's house, a nice detached villa in a country road along which were built a few council houses, a village shop and a recreation ground, was struck one night and completely demolished, everything being blown to smithereens except the WC which remained intact and standing upright on the pile of rubble which was once a home. Another bomb dived into a field on a hill, tunnelled under a road and came up inside a bungalow on the other side, blowing the occupants out of the window. Miraculously they were not killed, suffering only broken limbs and shock.

Barnet suffered slightly more damage being a larger town.

33

THE COALMAN'S HOUSE AFTER THE BOMB.

Alan returned to school one day to find part of the building had been struck, but as school was not in session at the time no one was hurt. Much to Alan's disgust the school was closed for one day only, then lessons continued as usual.

The night raids were the most frightening and before the Anderson Shelter was erected, I would lie in the double bed I shared with Cindy listening to the menacing sound of the enemy aircraft engines as they approached nearer and nearer, like a swarm of deadly bees, telling myself not to show how frightened I was for the sake of my eight year old sister, but to try to be brave for both of us. Like many others I never forgot my nightly prayer.

The raids on London by this time had become a daily and nightly occurrence as long as the weather stayed fine and clear, and that summer was particularly fine and clear of cloud. To begin with, as soon as the alert sounded our parents had hauled us out of bed to huddle under the shelter of the staircase in the centre of the house where we spent many hours sitting on pillows and cushions trying to doze when it was quiet, or making forays into the kitchen for a sustaining warm drink, but as the frequency of the raids increased we were all suffering from loss of sleep. So it was decided that we be allowed to stay in our beds as long as was possible and only when the action became too close and we heard the warning whistles of the wardens did we retreat to our hidy-hole under the stairs. This terrifying period of the war between August and October 1940 became known as the 'Battle of Britain', when London was bombed for fifty-seven consecutive nights and often by day also.

As war went on the raids increased in ferocity with bigger and bigger bombs. Hitler did his best to bomb London out of existence. After the all-clear signal had sounded on one occasion, my father took us outside to look at the sky in which there was a bright orange glow spreading for miles caused by the burning buildings of London's dockland and East End. Some nights we watched the strong yellow rays of the searchlights as they probed the sky with sharp fingers to find the attacking aircraft and pin-point it in a crossbeam of light

A QUIET NIGHT ?

and enable the ack-ack guns to target on it. When the raiders came in waves of hundreds, the flak from these guns was continuously exploding in bright flashes about them. The clatter of the guns, the buzz of aircraft, the whine and explosions of bombs, plus the bells of fire engines and ambulances all made for noisy nights, and we became so accustomed to this that on the nights when there was no activity we became suspicious of the quiet, not believing in our good fortune. People were getting such little sleep that the government issued free ear plugs to all who wanted them. I doubt if many accepted the offer. Most preferred to stay alert in order to cope with emergencies.

Once the air-raid shelter was erected our parents insisted we slept there every night while they made a bed up under the stairs for themselves. In the beginning we found it an adventure to have this little cave to ourselves and did not mind the primitive furnishings. My father left the oil lamp hanging from the roof on a low light so that we were never in complete darkness except for the night when a plane dropped a land-mine about half a mile away and the repercussions of the blast blew out the light and made the lamp swing wildly from its hook. The shaking brought Dad out to check that we were safe. We had been rudely awakened by the blast, but on this occasion it appeared to have been a lone raider who had sneaked through the defences without being seen, so no warning was given. Once he had dropped his deadly load he made off back to base and we had no more bombs. The land-mines were an escalation of the deadliness of the bombs dropped at the beginning of hostilities. They were more drumlike in shape than the conventional bombs and did far greater damage. They were dropped by parachute and just one land-mine could flatten a whole street of houses, the blast being felt over a very long distance, as we had experienced.

During daylight raids we had watched our pilots weaving patterns high in the sky as they attacked enemy planes trying to get through to London. When enemy fighter planes accom-panied the bombers dogfights would occur and although the planes were usually too high for us to distinguish any markings we all followed the aerial acrobatics performed and silently willed our men to win. When the raid was over and the skies cleared, boys searched the roads and gardens for spent bullets and shrapnel. These cartridge cases and pieces of heavy jagged metal were souvenirs of the time and some were kept for many years, but as time went on and the war continued, most of these boys were involved in the fighting themselves and lost their taste for such mementoes.

In these gigantic daylight raids during the month of August scores were kept of the number of aircraft shot down. These were broadcast next day on the wireless: for instance 13 August 1940 seventy-eight enemy planes were destroyed for the loss of three of our pilots, 14 August over one hundred and sixty-one enemy aircraft destroyed for the loss of thirty-four of our machines and eighteen pilots. On 15 and 16 August Rochester and Chatham were attacked. On 18 August Portsmouth was blasted and the score became one hundred and forty-one enemy planes shot down for ten pilots lost; and so it went on. On 20 August in his speech to the House of Commons, Winston Churchill paid tribute to Britain's RAF Fighter Force. These young pilots were mainly the product of the state secondary schools and proved their worth over Britain's skies. Churchill acknowledged this with his famous phrase, 'Never in the field of human conflict has so much been owed by so many to so few.'

During a raid in September 1940 Buckingham Palace was hit and Queen Elizabeth was reputed to have said, 'I can now look the East Enders in the eye', or words to that effect, for the East End of London had suffered fearful destruction, thousands killed and hundreds made homeless. The Royal Family remained in London throughout the worst of the Blitz, the King and Queen making unannounced and informal visits to some of the worst hit areas to see for themselves the devastation caused by the raids. Princess Elizabeth spoke on the wireless for the first time when she addressed the children of the country on 13 October 1940 in a 'Children's Hour' programme. I can remember listening with Alan and Cindy and thinking how clear her voice sounded then. These days no doubt her speech would be considered a trifle stilted.

Due mainly to the valiant efforts of the RAF, the Luftwaffe sustained such heavy losses that by November the daylight raids virtually ceased and Hitler concentrated on night raids of large forces of German fighter planes dropping bombs at random from a great height then departing rapidly before they could be intercepted. Birmingham, Swansea, Southampton, Bristol and Plymouth as well as London suffered from such strategy. In London a bomb went through the tower of Big Ben, but failed to stop the clock which continued to give the correct time and still chime the hours. Civil Defence workers were worn, blackened and haggard from sleepless nights and their toils among the many fires and fallen buildings. From 7 September 1940 to 13 January 1941 13,339 people in London had been killed and 17,937 severely injured. Hitler had expected the Blitz ('Blitz' taken from the German word *Blitzkrieg* meaning lightning war) to subdue the people of Britain, so that he and his followers would just walk in, but he had not bargained for the stubborn determination of the British character in its citizens. Churchill with some of his staff toured the bombed areas of Bristol City the morning after one of its worst night raids and was cheered by its tired, battered, but not dispirited people.

The ex-prime minister, Neville Chamberlain, died of cancer on 9 November 1940 and his funeral was held in the bomb-blasted building of Westminster Abbey with the cold wind piercing through its shattered windows. In Churchill's tribute to his predecessor given before the House of Commons in Church House, deemed safer at this time than Westminster, he said:

> 'The only guide to a man is his conscience. The only shield to his memory is the rectitude and sincerity of his actions. It is very imprudent to walk through life without this shield, because we are so often mocked by the failure of our hopes and the upsetting of our calculations; but with this shield, however the fates may play, we march always in the ranks of honour.'

On Christmas Day an unofficial truce prevailed and the night was a quiet one. The respite was short and the raids soon recommenced. Portsmouth becoming one of the targets. In London on 8 March 1941 the Café de Paris was hit and a hundred or more people dining and dancing there were trapped in the rubble of the building. There were many deaths. On 10–11 May a further 1,436 were killed and 1,752 injured.

One strange and unexpected apparition to drop out of the skies on 12 May 1941 was Hitler's friend and deputy Rudolf Hess. He was reported to have come on his own initiative with a proposal for terms of peace. He did not make much headway, but was locked away for the duration of the war.

On land, Allied forces under General Wavell had been gaining victories in North Africa over the Italian forces which *Il Duce*, Benito Mussolini, had brought into war against Britain. The Greeks also had their successes against Italian invaders of their land. At sea, although we lost many ships in the Atlantic there was a naval success against the Italian fleet off Cape Matapan. These were small points of light in an otherwise dark sky. Even these were obscured when strong German forces were sent to attack Yugoslavia and Greece and to strengthen the Axis troops in North Africa. In North Africa they advanced from Tripoli causing the Allies to retreat from ground they had taken. The Greek and Yugoslav armies surrendered, but those who could and wished to continue opposition took to the hills and continued their fight from there. Tito was one of those who with his group of communist supporters waged guerrilla warfare from the mountains of his homeland.

Crete was yet another territory to be invaded by Hitler's armies who parachuted into this mountainous island. Again our armies were forced to evacuate for Britain had no air cover to support them. We were still desperately short of aircraft and arms of all kinds.

HMS *Prince of Wales* and HMS *Hood* had found and attacked the German battleship *Bismarck*. In the attacking fire the *Hood* was sunk and *Bismarck* escaped only to be rediscovered and sunk three days later.

Closer to home all were shocked and horrified in October 1941 when our defences were penetrated by enemy submarines and the warship the *Royal Oak* was sunk while at anchor in Scapa Flow, Scotland.

Amongst all the turmoil, the death of the instigator of the First World War, Kaiser William II, on 4 June 1941 at Doorn in Holland, passed almost unnoticed and unmourned.

3

In the early years of the war when we were still in the process of adapting to the new conditions, small villages like Borehamwood were sometimes overwhelmed by the influx of large numbers of young men in uniform. These young men found little to do in their off-duty hours away from their camps. Apart from the weekly dance, the local cinema and pubs, there was not a great deal to entertain them. A few people who had been connected with stage productions in the entertainment world decided to do something about it and asked local residents to join them in producing a pantomime. Some friends of mine joined the group and with my parents permission I too was allowed to take part. *Alladin and His Wonderful Lamp* was the theme of the story, with many adaptations to suit the local cast. My part was a small one as one of the dancers and chorus. We had regular and quite tough rehearsals and for the first time I had experience of the work and trauma involved in producing a show on stage. Eventually, costumes, lighting, scenery, cast and music all came together and the pantomime was played nightly for one week to a packed audience in the local hall.

In 1941, when I was fifteen, I persuaded my parents, much against their will, to allow me to leave school and go to work. The job was that of a clerk with an insurance company, C T Bowring, evacuated from the city of London to share the premises of the film studios situated near to our home. Although I had always enjoyed school in the earlier years, it was a great relief to cast aside my school uniform and petty restrictions to join the adult world. The thrill and satisfaction of receiving my first pay packet of twenty-five shillings kept me in a happy glow for several days. After much thought I divided my money by giving five shillings to my mother towards my keep, putting aside five shillings for clothing and necessities, keeping five shillings for pocket money and the rest into Post Office savings until required for larger expenses. This seemed to work quite well as five shillings went a long way in those days.

My entry into the world of wage earners was enthusiastic and any little job I was given was done in double-quick time. When given messages to deliver, I raced down the corridors and back with the answers so quickly that my boss had difficulty in keeping me occupied. My office companions in the marine claims' section consisted of two married ladies and two other girls a year or so older than myself: all the men already having been called for the armed forces. One of the girls, Paddy, who although not endowed with great good looks, had a lively personality and a keen interest in classical music and whereas most girl's heart throbs came from the film world, her pin-up boy was a cellist whose movements and performances she followed with devotion.

Of the two married ladies Mrs B was short, rotund, cheerful and very kind as she did her best to explain to me the mysteries and complications of the mechanical calculating machine. This was worked by the rotation of a handle reminiscent of the old barrel organs. I never fully understood the ins and outs of the machine or even the various insurance claims on which we worked, but as long as I followed the set formula all seemed to be well.

Mrs F arrived in the office a month or two after myself. She was large, comfortably built and came from Manchester. Her regional accent was new to me and caused some amusement amongst all these southerners. She took it all in good humour and told us episodes of her family life in which her daughter Letitia figured often. Apart from the name, Letitia, which I had not come across before, I remember nothing more about her for we never met.

In charge of our section was Mr A , a smallish bespectacled man of pleasant disposition. He was an extremely heavy smoker whose breath, clothes and office reeked of nicotine. I

43

was extremely glad that he chose Joan and not myself to share his small room. He had suffered being gassed in the First World War and his cough could be heard through the thin walls of the office partition all hours of the day. His consumption of a vast number of cigarettes did nothing to alleviate his condition. We were not aware at that time of the connection between smoking and cancer.

Joan, the other young girl had been to the same school as me. We both lived in the village and knew the same people. We became friends and usually went for coffee and tea breaks together at the canteen which catered not only for personnel from the insurance company, but for all others working in the film studios as well.

Coming from a sheltered and strict Baptist background where 'blast' was a swear word, I was shocked and horrified at the loose language and endearments that slipped from the lips of these people so easily, but within a few weeks I grew to understand it meant little and accepted it as part of the artificial world in which they lived. It was not my world and although I found it interesting to observe I had no wish to join them. We occasionally saw the stars of the films and heard little bits of the gossip that surrounded them and realised that there were other aspects to these celluloid performers than those shown on the silver screen.

There were more young people working in other offices within the company, boys as well as girls. One of these boys took to walking past our office door about the time we were leaving to go home for lunch and when work was finished for the day. He and his friends also seemed to arrange their coffee breaks for the same time as Joan and I. Eventually they plucked up courage and spoke to us. Soon there was a group of six or more of us taking our coffee breaks together and our friendship developed to activities outside of work.

The lad who had first drawn our notice by his attention to our office, was tall, dark and cheerful. He appeared to have marked me as his partner in most of our meetings. He seemed to have signified this intent by laying in wait and making me his target one winter's day when snow lay inches deep on the ground, turning a mundane and not particularly attractive area into a brilliant white world. As Joan and I walked out of the building we were met by a volley of snowballs flying around us, some of which scored a hit. Recognising our assailants we determined to retaliate and the ensuing battle broke any ice there may have been and had us all laughing and breathless.

Gerry was just seventeen and came from a town ten miles from our village. He and his friends travelled in by train each day. As our friendship developed he missed a few trains on his return journey, but was never unduly late to cause concern to his family or mine. In the short daylight hours of winter, with problems of blackout and air-raids there were few places for young people to meet apart from their homes. Most meetings were in the company of groups when we braved the darkness of the blackout to travel to a dance or even a show in London. The evening we went to see *No No Nanette* was the very first time I had been to London without the company of my parents. I would have been completely at a loss as to which buses or trains to take and the addition of the blackout with its complete absence of light or illuminating signs confused me even more. Gerry was a most protective guide and steered me safely through the dark streets avoiding lamp posts and pedestrians which loomed up unexpectedly out of the blackness. Once we had negotiated the entrance to the underground train system, the brilliant lights dazzled our straining eyes and we travelled easily to our final station, before making another dive into darkness to reach the theatre doors.

Inside the building it was once more bright lights and cheerfulness. All were able to forget the problems of the times and lose themselves in the music and comedy of the show. I was enchanted to be in a London theatre with so many people. So much activity, so much sophistication was exhilarating. Away from the confines of the family, with my own friends, I felt free and daring. When the show ended we left the theatre in high spirits to make another foray into the blackout to find our way home. My friends seemed to be able to make even the blackest, coldest night into light-hearted fun.

Gerry had me safely returned to my parents by eleven

o'clock and after a warm drink and a clasp of hands, left to return to his own home. Boys, at least the well brought up ones, did not expect kisses and cuddles from their girlfriends until a friendship was firmly established and I would have felt surprised and alarmed if they had. My parents expected to meet any boyfriend I had before I was allowed out alone with him and our escorts were expected to collect and return us to our own front door, no matter how far they had to travel afterwards. I was seventeen before I received my first kiss from a boy and that single kiss was a great emotional experience which seemed to incur the most amazing internal reactions, which surprised me greatly by their unexpectedness. Mostly we found pleasure in friendship without complications involving deeper feelings.

My emotions were moved as were the emotions of many others by the film *Dangerous Moonlight* made in 1941, starring Anton Walbrook as a Polish pianist who had escaped from the devastation of Warsaw in order to bring the plight of Poland to the notice of the world through his music. The music, named the *Warsaw Concerto* composed for the film by Richard Addinsell, swept the country and brought a lump to the throat of most of those who heard it. The film and music did more to awake people to the awareness of what had happened than any prime minister's speech or newscast.

Hitler continued his *Blitzkrieg* and other cities apart from London were the recipients of his rage. Coventry, Exeter and Plymouth all suffered from his bombers' attention, the shopping centres of which were destroyed as also was the old cathedral of Coventry. The raids on the cathedral cities were known as the 'Baedekar raids.'

Mussolini, *Il Duce*, the strutting, comic-opera leader of Italy, joined Hitler in his attack on the Allied forces. France and the other allied Continental countries being overrun by Germany: Britain with the help of men from her dominions and those groups of Polish, Dutch, French and others who had escaped from their enemy-occupied lands were left to fight on alone in Europe.

The U S A , although not at war, was, with the help of

President Roosevelt, keeping us supplied with materials and badly needed equipment and our own workers were toiling long hours keeping production going, turning out planes, ships and guns to replace those lost and to increase the power of our fighting units. To finance the materials needed to continue our struggle, a Lease Lend Bill was passed by the USA government making funds available in return for bases for America in the West Indies.

On the home front, rations were tightened. The national loaf using whole grain flour was introduced and the white loaf using refined flour gradually disappeared from our shops. In the August of 1942 food rations were cut. Instead of the four ounces of butter per person we had been getting, the allowance was reduced to two ounces a week. Sugar was cut from twelve ounces to eight ounces and other items became more scarce. There were no onions except those you grew yourself. Dried eggs and Spam, a tinned meat substitute, were introduced. Canned food was already on points as were cereals. Cheese ration was two ounces, tea – two ounces, meat ration – one shilling two pennies a week and two pence in corned beef. Even common-place items became scarce and housewives spent long hours in queues to obtain food for the family. Such a mundane thing as a potato became in short supply, almost unbelievable to a country where they were a staple food. Those well-endowed with plenty of money were not so badly affected as it was still possible in the first few years of the war to buy a good unrationed meal at a restaurant, but eventually, although it was still possible to buy a meal at such an establishment, the menu was restricted to two courses by rule of Lord Woolton, Minister for Food. The poorer members of society did not have the means to exercise this choice, which caused some bitterness on their part.

People were urged to save paper and newspapers were reduced to four pages. Collections were made for bundles of cardboard, magazines and any other form of paper lying around in the house. Attics were searched and emptied which served a double purpose, the second being lessening the risk of fire. Sticky labels were sold to enable one to reuse the same envelopes again and again. When one finally had to renew the supply, the new envelopes were of a recycled paper, a mottled creamy brown in colour. Other items to be salvaged were metal goods. Wrought-iron gates, iron railings, old machinery, tools, anything made of metal and not absolutely necessary to life at that time, was collected and taken away to be melted down for the war effort, supposedly to be used to make more guns, tanks or aircraft. When the collectors came up our road they took the chains that hung between the brick posts and a number of aluminium saucepans my mother donated. Neighbours provided similar items. Many Regency and Edwardian houses lost their fine decorative wrought-iron work at this time which changed the appearance of many homes and terraces. Paper and metal were not the only items people were urged to save: there was a need for almost everything from bits of string to rags, bottles and bones. The string would help to make lining for aircraft, rags to make paper, the bottles could be reused and bones would make cordite, glue and fertilizer. The rag and bone man who came collecting up our road every few weeks with his horse and cart made a useful contribution to the nation's war efforts.

In 1942 petrol became vital to our continuing struggle and private motorists were banned from using it. When war was first declared motorists had been allowed six gallons a month. Other forms of fuel were tried. Some cars carried large inflated gas bags on their roofs as a substitute fuel, others tried various other smelly effluents, but most drivers resigned themselves to the inevitable and stowed away their cars for the duration of the war. At the beginning of hostilities all car drivers had been asked to immobilise their vehicles when parking by removing the distributor from their engine. This was to avoid its use by any possible invaders or unauthorised persons. I remember my mother driving we three children to St Albans town one day and parking in the market place whilst we went to do our shopping. On returning laden with various purchases which were packed into the car, we took our seats and Mother turned the key to start the engine. Nothing happened. Time and again she tried becoming more flustered and worried with every turn.

When this failed to draw any life from the engine she resorted to the cranking handle hoping that this would evoke some response. It was no use. By this time one or two gentlemen had appeared to offer their help, concerned for this lady in obvious distress and it was only when one of them raised the car bonnet to examine the engine that Mother remembered the distributor in her handbag. Covered in confusion and blushing furiously she produced the essential piece of equipment and apologised profusely to these gallant gentlemen before replacing this cause of the problem and making a hurried retreat home with a perfectly working engine.

Even water, especially hot water, did not escape the eye of the economisers. In 1942 everyone was requested to use no more than five inches of water in their bath at a time. This was probably in order to save on the electricity or fuel required to heat it. Posters and information films were displayed showing how to measure the required amount, or bringing this directive to one's notice in a more amusing illustrative manner. The well-publicised poster advertisement for shampoo in the 1930's 'Friday night is Amami night', still held good for many, but again required economy of hot water. Another poster showing the head of a handsome young RAF pilot with sleek, shining hair, advertising hair cream, was responsible for the nickname given to members of the RAF. From then on they were known among other service personnel as 'The Brylcream Boys'.

In June 1942 some young men were drafted to work in the coal mines to aid production which had fallen in the preceding year. Known as 'Bevin Boys' after Ernest Bevin the Minister of Labour, they were chosen by ballot and consequently came from a variety of backgrounds.

In order to make the most of all the daylight hours, in 1940 the government had introduced summer time or double summer time when the clocks were put forward or back an hour; forward in Spring and back in Autumn.

My father was having problems in his business, his un-married lady assistants were taken for war work in factories, sweets were rationed, cigarettes and tobacco in short supply and boxes of matches were almost extinct. He had to eke out his supplies to his regular customers on an 'under the counter' sort of system, which often caused unpleasant scenes from ill-tempered customers short on their nicotine quota. All the effects of addiction were very noticeable at times like that.

Even boys to deliver newspapers seemed to be few and far between that winter and to help out I took a round to deliver on my way to work. It was a severe winter both war and weatherwise. There was deep snow and many achingly cold frosty mornings, when our pre-central heating houses had windows obscured by glorious white crystal patterns of ferns and feathers framed by a deep fringe of icicles. Then only the strongest of will-power forced one from the warmth of bed. Clad in layers of warm clothing, pixiehood, scarf, woollen gloves and wellington boots, I sallied forth into a glistening white landscape, my sack of newsprint across my shoulders and my breath freezing before my eyes. To each customer's door I trudged with a folded copy of the latest news deemed suitable by the censor to reach the eyes and ears of the population. This I pushed through each letter-box, high or low, avoiding if possible the snapping return of the strong spring variety and the even snappier teeth of various little dogs who considered anyone carrying a sack an intruder on their territory. By the time my round was completed and I arrived at my place of work, all feeling had disappeared from feet, hands and face. As I tried to restore some warmth and movement into my fingers by holding my hands over the radiators heating the office, pain engulfed every nerve for ten minutes or more until circulation was fully restored. This confirmed my suspicion that all Arctic explorers were not only brave, but mad too!

Sweets were among the items rationed and not only rationed, but very hard to come by, even with the necessary coupons. Retailers were strictly limited in the amount they were allocated and this allocation scarcely lasted more than two or three days. Then another week would go by before the next supply arrived. Knowing when goods were going to be available was important as even the most ordinary items became more scarce. Queues formed as soon as the shopkeeper started to unpack a box. There was no point in waiting for goods to be displayed, you would have been too late to obtain anything then. Queuing became compulsory in April 1942 and has remained with us as a polite habit. Housewives frequently joined queues without knowing what they were queuing for and if there happened to be a couple of oranges at the end of a fifteen minute wait, that was well worthwhile. Oranges were available for children only. For this reason I was popular among my workmates, as I was in the know when it came to confectionery. Every two weeks I collected ration books from my colleagues and took them home when I went to lunch. The ration in July 1942 was limited to two ounces per person per week. Mother would have the required number of sweets ready, already weighed and wrapped in paper bags. I handed over the books, Mother cut out the vital coupons and after lunch I returned to work with the goods to be greeted with gurgles and cries of joy from my sugar-starved, mouthwatering workmates who were only too pleased to hand over the necessary cash. My friends enjoyed this little luxury in various ways. Some opened their bags of delight and dived straight in to slake their craving; the strong-minded ones put theirs aside to enjoy the pleasure at leisure during the evening; the really strong-willed among them rationed out their ounces of ecstasy over the next few days. All enjoyed the afternoon in happy anticipation, or sucking complacency, prolonging the tasteful contents as long as possible.

To add to my parent's problems, early in 1941 my mother became pregnant once more. Like most pregnancies of those days it was unplanned and in this case unwelcomed as my parents felt there were enough difficulties to contend with at the time. With raids, rations and business worries along with the three growing youngsters they already had, another pregnancy was just too much to bear. However, bear it she did right through the full nine months only to have a still-born birth at the end of that period. This was even more distressing for her. Whether it was the tension of the continual raids which harried us every night and necessitated her rolling out of her bed and under it for protection from the falling bombs, or the fact that in the ninth month of her pregnancy, Prince, our

51

cocker spaniel excitedly jumped up at her one day, the reason is uncertain, but it caused my mother a very unhappy year. During the latter part of this time Cindy went to stay with an aunt and uncle in Surrey, leaving Alan and myself with our parents. Alan and I were not fully aware of the implications of 'having a baby' and neither of us were duly concerned when mother came home without one. Although I had been helping her to crochet tiny matinée jackets and other small garments, I was unable to visualise the small creature they were intended for. Looking back on that time we must have seemed rather heartless in that we could not mourn with my mother for our tiny brother.

For the young people of the village there were various organisations, run by worthy volunteers, in which to spend some of their free time. The Boy Scouts, Girl Guides, (of which I was a member up until the age of fourteen or so), a number of youth clubs, mostly connected with the churches and the Air Training Corps for boys. There was no comparable organisation for the female young until the Girls' Training Corps was formed in 1942 when I was sixteen. It was set up to cater for girls of sixteen and upwards and filled the gap between leaving school and eighteen years of age when every young person was either called up for one of the services or drafted into other forms of war work. My girlfriends and I became founder members of the GTC in our village and wore the uniform with pride. In our navy blue skirts, white blouses and navy forage caps, we felt that we were recognised as being capable of playing a part in the defence of our country and were all eager to do so. Our first lessons consisted of being taught to march in formation, right turn, left turn, and turn about, without tripping one another up. When we were reasonably good at obeying orders we were encouraged to take a turn at giving them and drill each other. Those of us who were successful gained a stripe and became section leaders.

Other lessons were given in aircraft recognition, map work, despatch carrying, first-aid and fieldcraft by people qualified as tutors in such subjects. On one fieldcraft exercise we were all sent out from the secondary school in which our meetings were

NOBODY HAD NOTICED WE WERE MISSING!

held into the surrounding area and told to make our way back without being seen by guards standing at the gates. The school stood on a hill with a steep slope running down from the opposite edge of the road before the gate. This grass covered slope provided various bushes and groups of brambles which a friend and I thought would make good cover. So having crawled along the ditch at the base we gradually worked our way up the slope taking advantage of the bushes, mostly crawling on all fours, or flat on our stomachs, to the gateway of the school. When we reached the entrance we found to our surprise that it was unguarded. Puzzled by this we cautiously made our way in, grubby and scratched, to find everyone enjoying a refreshment break having given up the exercise ten minutes earlier. No-one appeared to have noticed that we were still missing!

There were of course social activities connected with the GTC and together with members of the ATC we organised dances and concerts. Some of the young people had formed small band groups and were able to provide music for these occasions. I have memories of trying to teach my brother to dance by guiding him around the living room floor to the strains of Victor Sylvester's orchestra issuing from the old wireless set and to the detriment of my toes, but we managed a passable waltz between us. The concerts were performed for the local population and some for the members of the forces who were patients in a nearby hospital. It kept us happily occupied, out of mischief, and we found it all great fun.

A netball team was formed in which I was the shooter and most of our Saturdays were spent playing league matches against teams from other areas. We also had one practise evening each week. We neither had nor wanted such things as television or discos; our interests kept us active and busy.

By the time I was seventeen I was leading a very full life; working for the insurance company during the day and immediately going from there to help my father in his shop, as he was by now desperately short of assistants; then in the evenings I kept a busy social life with the GTC activities, singing lessons and singing commitments with various groups at evening entertainments. Although I had always felt rather shy and been somewhat reserved in my attitude toward strangers, my nervousness disappeared when I sang, and I had no hesitation in performing before a large number of people when asked. Friends of both sexes from my village, school and work filled any other spare hours and we managed to enjoy ourselves in spite of bombing and wartime restrictions. We were lucky in having few responsibilities, but for our parents it was different and the furrows on their brows increased along with the problems.

As they reached the age of eighteen, the boys from our circle of friends left the village to enlist in one of the armed services and were sent to various stations in Britain and abroad. They reappeared at infrequent intervals, smart and assured in their uniforms for a reunion with their friends still remaining in the village and hoping to find a girlfriend available to escort to the weekly dance. I found myself called upon to indulge in this pleasant duty at very short notice on more than one occasion. My parents never had any fears for me at these times as they were all lads I had grown up with, whom they knew well and who respected their standards. Few people kept late nights and most activities closed down by eleven p.m; only on special occasions did any dance or entertainment continue past that hour. Normally, I was expected to be home by ten o'clock; in the case of a dance in company with someone they trusted, permission was given to remain until the last waltz. Consequently I was seen to be escorted by a partner in khaki one week, air force blue a week or two later and navy blue at other times, all of whom met my parents when they collected me from my home and afterwards returned me to my front door, with a few words of thanks for the evening, a handclasp and a friendly goodnight. Of the boys in our road, one joined a tank regiment and most of the others went into the RAF, having been keen members of the ATC. One became a dog handler, and was posted to Palestine. At my brother's school almost the entire sixth form joined the Fleet Air Arm as soon as they were able and sad to say many never returned, my friend's brother amongst them.

My brother at the age of seven had decided he wanted to be a sailor and when he was fifteen he left the grammar school to go to nautical college in London. Gerry had also decided to be a sailor and at eighteen joined The Royal Navy. We continued to be friends and kept up a correspondence. Whenever he was on leave he came to see me, being accepted as one of the family when he was home. In his bell-bottomed trousers, wide collar and round cap perched on the back of his curly head, he looked every inch the jaunty sailor boy, cheerful and humorous. I was taken to meet his family and friends in St Albans and every moment of his leave when I was free was spent together. In this way I was accepted as his regular girlfriend and he as my regular boy, with my parents' approval. It was not long before Gerry, a signaller or 'bunting tosser' in naval slang, was posted to the Orkney Islands and Scapa Flow, a remote outpost of Britain where his opportunities for home leave were strictly limited. Instead, fat envelopes containing long amusing letters regularly dropped through our letter box each week and equally long letters were written and dispatched to Scapa Flow, giving news of mutual friends, work and life in the village. All service mail was censored before sending and frequently arrived at their destination with blacked out spaces where a forbidden name or detail had been mentioned. At least one censor was not a fan of Tommy Handley and the ITMA show, the most popular radio show of the time, as on one occasion Gerry had signed off his letter with T T F N (Ta Ta For Now) a catchphrase from the show. The censor had blacked it out, no doubt imagining it to be a secret code giving information to the enemy. In some cases it was wise to write on only one side of the paper as some censors actually went to the trouble of cutting out words which might give helpful information to enemy agents, and letters could arrive looking more like paper doilies than correspondence. Any details appertaining to troop movements, equipment, names of vessels, units, places etc. had to be avoided or were deleted, and even quite innocent remarks or phrases such as the T T F N were removed if the censor felt them to be suspicious.

Correspondence played a big part in keeping up the morale

of the men and women away from home. There were often requests from men abroad to girls at home to find a pen-friend for a pal who received little mail. In this way I started a correspondence with Jack, a lance-corporal in the Eighth Army then fighting in North Africa. This section of our army was among those nicknamed the Desert Rats because of the long spell of fighting they underwent in the sands of North Africa. Our subjects for writing were limited by several factors. One, we had never met; two, we had no mutual friends; three, the conditions in which he was living; and four, the censor, of course. However, we were able to write about ourselves, our likes and dislikes, and what we hoped to do in the future. I also tried to include some amusing incident that had occurred during the week, small events that happened at work or with my activities with the GTC. Photographs were exchanged with our first few letters and I received one showing a fair-haired young man, dressed in army tropical uniform and with a tanned and cheerful face. In this way our weekly letters continued over a period of three or four years.

4

Fashions were simple in the 1940s. There was no choice, no frills or fripperies on which to spend your money. All clothes and materials cost not only money, but coupons. A mackintosh (raincoat) or other coat over twenty-eight inches long and lined was valued at fourteen coupons for a woman and sixteen for a man, an unlined mackintosh for a man was nine. A pair of boots or shoes, five coupons for women and seven for men; a pair of pyjamas for either sex cost eight coupons; petticoat, slip, combinations or cami-knickers cost four coupons; men's pants, vest or bathing costume cost the same number. A pair of stockings took two coupons and men's socks three. Even handkerchiefs cost one coupon for two. Children's clothes cost fewer coupons, but with continuing growth they of course required more clothes. Mothers bought larger sizes and adjusted hems etc. as the children grew. Each person was issued with a clothing book attached to their ration book which had to be detached and name, address and national registration number added before use. It contained sixty-six coupons per year as from June 1941 and these had also to cover household items such as towels, tablecloths and curtains, so every piece in one's wardrobe was made over, turned around and inside out. Mother's clothes were cut down for growing children, odd leftovers from fabrics inserted to make multi-coloured pleats, contrasting bodices, collars and even sleeves. Bits of braid disguised let down hems and other ingenious ideas were used to refreshen old garments. Undies were made from discarded parachute material if you could find it (not on coupons). Cheesecloth, scarce but unrationed, also found many uses apart from cheese making. Even flour bags and

58

sugar bags were well-washed, dyed and put into use in other ways. Old curtains and bits of left-over furnishing material were used to furnish the body rather than the room. Outgrown jumpers, pullovers and cardigans were unravelled and re-knitted. The old saying 'Necessity is the mother of invention', certainly came to life in the austerity of wartime.

Manufactured 'utility' clothing was introduced in 1942. Skirts were shortened to knee length, pleats and fullness simplified to a new slim line showing neat figures to advantage and flattering the not so neat. Undies were minus lace, trousers minus turnups. Women made overcoats from blankets and there was a thriving market in second-hand clothes and goods. The WVS ran a useful exchange system giving points on those items given in and deducting points for those taken out.

Stockings in pre-nylon days were made of lisle, rayon, artificial silk and silk, the artificial silk and silk varieties being as scarce as gold-dust. Many girls resorted to painting their legs with a liquid make-up and pencilling in a seam down the back of the legs to simulate the real thing. It was a great day for me when I received a parcel from Ken who was fighting in Italy, enclosing two pairs of real silk stockings, the only drawback being that the censor had been overgenerous with his blue stamp and the ink had seeped through and marked the silk. This did not stop me wearing them.

During the cold weather and chilly nights some people kept warm with the aid of a new style of costume made fashionable by Winston Churchill. Called a siren suit it was made in warm material and resembled a baggy all in one overall suit closely drawn around wrists and ankles and zipped up at the front, a cosy and quick garment in which to dress during night air raids; hence its name.

Mother and I made most of the clothes needed for ourselves and Cindy. We were particularly pleased with one pattern we found which gave the impression of a pleated skirt, but actually used less than one yard of material, all done by clever cutting and stitching. My father had a reasonable stock to keep him going for a year or two, but Alan, who at thirteen was shooting up out of his clothes, was our biggest problem. Precious coupons had to be spent to keep him in a decent state of dress. Some of these problems were eased when Alan at the age of sixteen became an apprentice officer in the merchant navy and joined his first ship. He was issued with special coupons for his uniform and mother no longer had the problem of keeping him clothed.

Clothes rationing continued until 1949, which denied a whole generation of young people the chance to express their personalities in any flamboyant extremes of dress. Colours during those years were also fairly subdued as dyes were limited, most being used for the various uniforms required during the years of war. Also, any strong colour dyes were not always colour-fast, some being inclined to run when washed or even caught in the rain.

Mother was a clever needlewoman, able to knit, crochet and sew. I still retain items she made: a tablecloth with a crochet border depicting cups and saucers, teapots and sugar bowls; other tablecloths and cushion covers she had embroidered with coloured silks and others embroidered in wool. Mother made sure that both her daughters knew how to do all these things and her lessons have proved of great benefit to us both. I have tried, and to some extent, succeeded in passing on some of these skills to my three daughters and trust they will also encourage similar skills in my grand-daughters.

When I started to set up my own home in 1946, some household linen was almost unobtainable. I remember making a table-cloth by stitching together several large white handkerchiefs which I embroidered with a simple border pattern. It served its purpose as a small tea table-cloth until I was able to replace it with the real thing. Although some curtaining was still available, I could not afford the coupons it would cost, but I badly needed curtains for the bedroom window. Instead, I begged any odd scraps of material from my mother, aunts and friends and spent many hours feather-stitching the pieces together to make patchwork lengths of suitable size for my windows. They may not have been a great work of art, but the finished curtains gave the necessary screen and brightened the room considerably with their multi-colours and patterns.

Waking each day to see this splash of bright colour in the light of morning gave me great satisfaction, a feeling of achievement in producing something useful and attractive from so little. I could appreciate the pride those early pioneer women of America must have felt when they had completed the making of a patchwork quilt, the longing for colour and beauty which was expressed in their work and often denied them in their utilitarian circumstances.

Cosmetics were also few and far between in those years of war. I used little apart from lipstick, but I seem to recall that the fashion involved a rather heavy make-up over some of the period. Perhaps it was just a case of putting on 'a brave face' on the part of women. My straight hair was curled either by rolling and tying the tresses in strips of rag, or by heating a pair of metal tongs over the burners of the gas stove and twisting my hair around them. Many times the acrid smell of burning hair filled the kitchen when I forgot to test the heat on a sheet of paper first, and then the length of my hair became an inch or two shorter. Pipe cleaners had been another means of producing curls, but they soon disappeared when shortages began and those which remained were jealously guarded by my father. Youthful vanity could ignore all discomforts for the sake of a head full of softly waving curls. The completed hairstyle could be tied back with ribbon, or held in place with an Alice band often made from celluloid, an early form of plastic. Another hair style in fashion at the time was the 'Edwardian'. I rather fancied this style, believing it suited my face and added an inch or two to my height, but I had trouble trying to keep my soft fine hair in place. There were no convenient hair sprays in those days. The 'page boy' was another popular style, slightly easier to manage. In this style, most of the hair was straight with the ends turned under into a soft roll usually just above shoulder length. I assume the fashion simulated the hairstyles depicted on pictures of court page-boys in days of old. Sometimes the hair was rolled back from the face and the roll secured with hair-grips (kirby-grips) or upswept at the sides and fastened in the same way, but leaving the remaining tresses to hang around the head in soft waves and curled ends.

I did not have my first permanent wave until a few weeks before my marriage. 'Perms' in the 1940s' required courage. The machines were cumbersome and caused the client excruciating discomfort. A permanent wave required the customer's hair to be rolled into tight curls over metal rollers, each roller being surrounded with a rubber pad. The permanent wave machine was then wheeled into position so that the saucer-shaped hood stood above the customer's head. Wires protruding from this hood were then clipped on to each roller and the electric machine switched on. The client was forced to remain in an uncomfortable upright position, unable to turn the head in any direction for the next hour. After this time the head would feel well and truly cooked. The machine was then switched off, the wires disconnected and the rollers and rubber pads removed. I know I was extremely disappointed that after having been through this ordeal, the resulting hairstyle produced a dry, wavy frizz resembling straw rather than hair. My naturally sleek and shiny locks had gone. It was many years before I was tempted to try another 'perm'.

My friend Joan who was a year older than myself had left work to join the WRNS in 1943. She made a visit to the office on her first leave, smart and efficient-looking in her new navy uniform and little round hat. With all my friends going I was also keen to get into uniform and be seen to be playing a part in winning this war. For even in the darkest days when we were suffering setback after setback, when one after another Norway, Denmark, Holland, Belgium and France were occupied by enemy forces, there was no talk of surrender. It might take a long time, but we had no doubt that we would win in the end. I once remarked to Ken that I would like to learn how to handle a gun. He was horrified at the idea, but when I pointed out to him that should the Nazis attempt to invade and occupy Britain, every able-bodied person ought to be able to put up a defence. He conceded the point. His reaction was shared by those in command and the nearest any of the women's services ever came to handling weapons was in the making, cleaning and maintenance of them. Even those members of the ATS on ack-ack duty were not allowed actually to fire the guns, although they manipulated the range finders to pin-point the targets and dealt with most of the other details necessary to activate the weapon. The ATS members of the ack-ack batteries also manned the highly secret radar units. The women were obliged to take their turn at guard duty, but instead of rifles they were issued with officer's batons or sticks. With these in place of a rifle they were put through all the drill of presenting arms and necessary guard procedure. Then holding their little stick they were sent to stand sentry against all unwelcome visitors.

Such an attitude seems strange these days, when in countries in the Middle East and Russia women have taken an equal part in the fighting. However, I am of course glad that I never had to put that wish into action, for as it was Hitler turned from invading Britain and in June 1941 attacked Russia instead. With the enemy's main thrust directed at Russia, the pressure on Britain eased a little and provided a short breathing-space. Although not officially at war, the government of the United States of America was sympathetic to our struggle, keeping us going with supplies of goods and materials, also providing loans of money with which to pay for them, in exchange for concessions in the West Indies. To begin with many ships and supplies were lost due to action by the packs of U-boat (*Unterdersee boats*) submarines which roamed the seas like ravaging wolves, but gradually the Royal Navy was equipped to fight back and protect the convoys carrying these vital needs. In April 1941 the USA had extended its patrol area of the North Atlantic. This helped to ease the burden of the Royal Navy who had a vast area to cover and protect with insufficient vessels.

When Russia became an ally of Britain, putting up a tough resistance against the German invasion, they too were desperately in need of supplies. British ships sailed through the dreadfully dangerous waters of the Arctic in order to take what was required to keep them fighting and, again, many of our sailors and vessels were lost in those icy seas. The book by Godfrey Winn *P Q 17* tells the story of one such convoy.

Although our radio news may not have told us all the facts,

we heard enough to know the seriousness of the situation. To add to our troubles Japan had joined the Axis powers and attacked Britain's possessions in the Far East. Hong Kong fell in December 1941. Completely unprepared, Malaya was overrun. Penang in the north of Malaya was taken in December 1941 and on 15 February 1942 Singapore fell. The few thousand raw troops only recently and much too lately landed were captured or killed without much chance of a fight, along with their Australian comrades who had been sent to the region. Two of our biggest battleships, HMS *Repulse* and HMS *Prince of Wales*, were sunk off the east coast of Malaya with a great loss of life. Burma was taken by the enemy and news began to filter through of Japanese atrocities on soldiers and civilians alike and the whole war situation from our point of view looked very black indeed.

In December 1941, Japan, carried away with their successes, had, without any warning or declaration of war, attacked the USA naval base, Pearl Harbour, on the island of Hawaii, crippling the US fleet and killing many people. This action had enraged the whole of the population of the United States of America and roused them to declare war against Japan, bringing the vast resources of that huge country into the war effort on our side. The British Empire was then no longer alone in its struggle.

At home events continued to be grim. Canterbury was bombed severely for the third time in the October of 1942 and the Duke of Kent, the King's brother, was killed in a plane crash on 25 August 1942. Later that year a ray of hope shone through this dark period when we heard landings of American troops had taken place along the North African Coast and on Sunday 15 November 1942 church bells were rung all over Britain to celebrate the allies victory in Libya at El Alamein.

By Christmas 1942, stocks were very low and goods almost depleted. Many food items were scarce and housewives were hard put to provide Christmas festivities. The Ministry of Food published various recipes on how to cook without fat; how to cook without eggs; hot dishes from corned beef; how to fry fish with very little fat and so on.

Here is an example of a utility cake recipe requiring no eggs and no milk:

'Put into a pan one breakfast cup of water,
one breakfast cup of sugar,
one breakfast cup of fruit,
a quarter of a pound of margarine,
a teaspoon of spice.
Boil for three minutes and let it cool.
Add a teaspoonful of bicarbonate of soda,
dissolved in a teaspoonful of hot water, and
add two and a half breakfast cups of self-raising
flour. Put in a greased tin and
bake for one and a half hours'

One would probably go butterless on bread and sugarless in tea, but one would have a cake!

As various ingredients and materials became difficult to obtain, substitutes were invented such as dried egg and dried milk. Substitutes for coffee or rubber and other items were used. Borrowing the German term we called them *ersatz* coffee or *ersatz* rubber. They did not taste or smell quite like the real thing, but they saw us through.

With the egg shortage came the popular song:

'Hey little hen, when, when, when,
Will you lay me an egg for my tea'.
Hey little hen, when, when, when,
Will you try to supply one for me. . .'

Other recipes gave hints on making a meatless pie, how to make light pastry in spite of dark flour; how to 'extend' margarine by adding a little plain flour, a pinch of salt and some milk; how to make bread pudding without fat; and how to make potatoes go further by mashing and mixing with dried egg, dried milk moistened, shaped into small rounds and fried or baked! Many of these recipes were surprisingly good and helped the harassed housewife to feed her family.

During these days of shortages a new poster appeared with a funny little character named Chad. Chad was shown behind a brick wall, the only visible part of him being the nose, eyes, top of bald head and fingers gripping the wall. Underneath would be printed 'Wot! No beer?' or 'Wot! No potatoes?' or some other commodity in short supply. The posters raised a wry chuckle. It was not long before Chad had caught the public's sense of humour and one could see Chads chalked up on walls and boards with their own particular message all over town.

As the young men we knew volunteered or were called up and left the village, they were replaced by others whose homes were in other parts of Britain, or even other countries, and who had been sent to our area for training or service. Those friends from the village or school who had elected to join the RAF to fly were, in their turn, sent to places like Canada and Southern Rhodesia (now Zimbabwe) for their training. Friendships were formed between the strangers and local girls, some developing into marriage. I formed no romantic attachments, but was glad of a boy or two to partner me at dances and act as escort. Before this could happen I had to overcome my father's fears and prejudice. No doubt memories of experiences in the First World War were behind his decree that no daughter of his would be allowed out with a soldier. Since every young man of a suitable age was by then a soldier, sailor or airman, it was a bleak prospect for me. My mother and I pointed out this fact to him and after meeting one or two of my new friends he relented and even welcomed them.

Ken was one of these young men, extremely shy and quiet and a little lonely. He loved the countryside and enjoyed writing poetry. He and I took our cocker spaniel, Prince, for long walks through the fields and woods which surrounded the village. My father had no reason to fear for my reputation as Ken was too shy even to hold my hand and our walks were models of decorum on which I did most of the chatting or we walked in silence. When his unit was moved on, Ken wrote long letters to me to which I duly replied and another long correspondence was started.

Many of the new influx of strange young men were looked

upon with curiosity on the part of the local inhabitants. Their accents were often strange to these residents of Hertfordshire and sometimes difficult to understand, particularly those from overseas. Among the newcomers were men from the north, south, east and west of our own country, also Poles, Czechs, French, Irish, Canadians and Australians, all with their broken or twangy English. Once two coachloads of RAAF (Royal Australian Air Force) in their darker blue uniforms suddenly arrived at the film studios in a boisterous and noisy fashion, soon making their presence known to all and sundry. Working in our office, my colleagues and I wondered at all these strange voices, quite unlike any accents we had heard before, and looked out of our window to see what was happening. As soon as we were spotted we became the recipients of good-natured but bold remarks and had to withdraw with blushing cheeks. This was our very first encounter with our Australian colonial cousins; brash and bold, yet likable, they bulldozed their way through British reserve.

The more unpleasant aspects of the war were always with us and we came to accept them as a part of our daily life. Frequently after raids, roads would be closed due to the presence of an unexploded bomb, called UXB for shortness, and it was necessary to make a detour to reach one's work place. Many of these bombs were of monster size, taking time to defuse and remove. In the meantime traffic and pedestrians had to find other routes. Odd incidents occurred which gave us an unexpected fright or shock. These left us a little shaken for a short while before we continued with our daily tasks. Once Alan and I were walking home with a friend when we heard a plane's engine and then the whining whistle of a bomb above us. We threw ourselves to the ground as there was no time to find further protection. The bomb buried itself in the earth about half a mile away with a loud 'krr-ump' sound. We expected to hear a whole series of whistles as the bombs usually arrived in strings of half a dozen or more with intervals of only seconds between each one. There had been no air-raid warning and as we lay there waiting for further explosions we realised

67

the sound of aircraft engines was fading and there appeared to be no further bombs falling. It must have been a lone raider releasing the last of its load before returning to base. It was not until we picked ourselves up and looked around us that we discovered we had thrown ourselves down in front of the local Co-op's large plate-glass window. If it had shattered in the blast it could have made a nasty mess of all three of us.

Another time I was returning to work after lunch when I saw a Spitfire fighter plane above me. Its engine sounded odd and the pilot seemed to be in trouble. As I watched, the plane suddenly dived towards earth and crashed about three miles away. Within minutes ambulances and fire engines were racing in that direction. I continued to the office white-faced and shaken. We heard later that the plane had crashed in a field behind a public house on Elstree hill and that sadly, the young Polish pilot was killed.

On the whole our village was lucky in escaping the dreadful havoc which was created in the cities and ports of Britain. At one particular period in the war our fighter pilots like 'Cat's Eyes Cunningham' seemed to be having great success in finding and attacking enemy aircraft raiding Britain under cover of night. It was put about by the government propaganda that the reason for this was the large amount of carrots our pilots ate which so improved their eyesight and people were encouraged to eat more carrots. In reality it was the discovery and invention of radar which was responsible and which the government wished to keep a secret from the enemy.

5

In the summer of 1943 Mother took Alan, Cindy and me for a holiday to Hunstanton in Norfolk, leaving my father to run the business with the aid of his assistant manager and part-time helpers. The town of Hunstanton is a small holiday resort which stands upon its distinctive red and white cliffs on the northern coast of Norfolk. In 1943 its tall Victorian terrace houses surrounding an open, sloping greensward overlooking the sea, its cliffside gardens and walks, well-maintained and flower bedecked in peacetime, had a neglected air. However, its sandy beaches were free of barbed wire entanglements and children were at liberty to build their castles in the sand or play in the small rocky pools. It was still possible to take a stroll along the promenade and watch the seagulls swirling in the summer sky.

There were few holidaymakers, even in July, instead the town was full of Canadian troops. Detachments of the Perth Regiment and the Gordon Highlanders from Nova Scotia in their Tam O'Shanters with a red bobble, were billeted throughout the town. They seemed to outnumber the resident population. I had heard a lot about Canada from my father who had spent some of his younger years working his way across this huge country and he still held a great affection for the land and its people. These young soldiers were far from shy and soon made themselves known to all the girls. Mother and I had gone to the sea-front to enjoy our first breath of salt air since 1939 and I had taken my sandals off to walk barefoot on the sand and look for shells. I had walked along a stretch of the beach and was washing my feet in a rocky pool before replacing my sandals when two young soldiers came dashing up and insisted upon helping me, one holding my sandal while the other supported me in balancing, all quite unnecessary, but they were unconvinced. My mother watched the episode with quiet amusement. My gallant helpers continued to chat in a friendly way and I suggested they might like to chat to my mother as well. I thought this might detract their interest, but no, they escorted me back to my mother on the promenade and she was also included in their friendly attentions.

Both young men were about nineteen or twenty years of age. One named Louis was a brown-eyed, stockily built French-Canadian with an attractive accent. The other, Pat, was a tall blond giant of Irish extraction with a fascinating soft Canadian drawl. These were the first Canadians I had ever spoken to and was intrigued by their speech. They had not been in Britain very long and told us that from the way the war was going they had expected to have to fight their way onto our beaches and were amazed that Britain had managed to hold out against Hitler's onslaught. We saw both young men frequently during our stay in Hunstanton and met many others besides. It was the practice of some of the soldiers to gather on the green in the summer evenings and sing to the accompaniment of a guitar played by one of their comrades. My brother and I joined them and before long I was asked to sing for them. The air-raids and war seemed to be only a bad dream in those idyllic, warm, light summer evenings. A relaxed and contented atmosphere pervaded that part of the town. Even when the sun finally went down, the bright moon took its place reflecting its light from the quiet surface of the sea below us and ignoring all blackout regulations.

The boarding house in which we stayed was one of a terrace of houses facing the cinema building. From the interior of this building Bing Crosby could be heard three or four times a day crooning the strains of the song 'I'm dreaming of a white Christmas' into the hot summer air. Several soldiers of the Perth regiment were billeted next door to the boarding house and had come to know some of the guests. In their off-duty time they could be found sitting on the cool grass chatting together. Some were homesick and liked to talk about their families and

SING - SONG ON THE GREEN

71

places from whence they came. I remember one soldier who wistfully extolled the beauty of the Canadian season of fall and the loveliness of the maple leaves changing colours. Amongst these men was one very quiet young boy who said little but, I noticed, watched me, giving me a shy smile when I caught his eye. Some of the older men teased him in a friendly fashion and he was emboldened to ask me to go to the cinema with him. Before I knew what was happening the 'date' was organised by his friends who were keen to inform me of the virtues of this bashful young man and who obviously were all too eager to pair us up. Don seemed a nice lad, the cinema was just across the road, and I hadn't seen the film before, so I eventually agreed and we duly 'went to the pictures'.

I must have been very naive in those days. Not quite eighteen, my experience was strictly limited to those boys I had grown up with or, like Gerry, I met in the course of my work, all of whom treated me with the greatest respect and took no liberties. I believe it was this complete innocence of any untoward sexual behaviour that carried me through my contacts with men of other cultural backgrounds unscathed. If any improper suggestions were made I simply did not understand them. As far as I was concerned, 'going to the pictures' meant just that: that both I and the boy concerned wished to see that particular film. Therefore when Don's arm started to creep around my shoulders I was a little surprised, but took no further notice as I was interested in the documentary film being shown at that moment. The film showed Cape Town, South Africa. I was writing to friends living there and would have been living there myself had my parents plans for our evacuation gone through. Poor Don, he had probably had to steel himself to overcome his shyness and then met with unresponsiveness and even indifference on my part. After a while the arm was withdrawn and we watched the film with only an occasional word of comment between us. After that episode we met once or twice to chat, usually with his friends around, but there were no more romantic overtures.

My holiday was kept fully occupied with other companions, among them Louis and Pat, and with my mother, brother and sister enjoying the countryside and pleasures that Hunstanton had to offer, and then in the evening joining in the singsong on the green. Whenever I hear the song 'You are my sunshine, my only sunshine', my thoughts wing back to 1943 and I see again those healthy young Canadian soldiers reclining on the grass in the warm evening twilight, joined by a few holidaymakers like ourselves, all relaxed and at ease singing the popular songs and ballads of the day to the accompaniment of the guitar and the soft sound of the lapping waves on the sandy beach.

We often wondered what happened to these cheerful young men, for we never saw them again, except for one, the guitar player. On the return home of my mother, Cindy and myself, my father joined my brother in Hunstanton for his holiday. A few days later he wrote to say that the guitar player had broken his leg and was in hospital near Watford. Dad enclosed the man's name and hospital address and suggested we might like to visit him. This was not an unusual thing to do as it was all part of the civilian war effort to welcome, host and generally help to make the members of the forces of the various dominions feel at home in Britain. The efforts were reciprocated when British lads were sent to the various dominions for training.

Mother was agreeable, so once a week we made a long bus ride out to the hospital where Jim was a patient, taking him small gifts to ease his stay. With shortages and rationing it was not easy to find much in the way of comforts for those in hospital, but we could provide books and magazines. In actual fact the Canadian troops were well cared for. A whole section of the hospital had been made over to them with their own compatriot doctors and nurses. Canada also provided all their supplies and equipment so there was little we could offer except our friendship.

Jim and I did not know one another very well and with my shyness and his disadvantage of being confined to bed, talk was a little stilted at first. Mother considered herself there as my chaperon and did not offer much in the way of conversation. I think she was also a little overcome at the vastness of this long low-roofed ward and its many male occupants. We were all

73

grateful for the large mugs of tea brought to us by a smiling nurse. Our visits continued through Autumn and Winter, for Jim in using his crutches managed to fall and break his leg for a second time.

During this time events were moving towards changes in our family circumstances. From April 1942 all girls reaching the age of sixteen were required to register and were issued with identity cards. As with all young people I had had to register in preparation for some sort of war service, for conscription of women had been introduced in the December of 1941. Many women had already taken over jobs normally done by men, such as bus conductors, porters, ambulance drivers, postmen, welders, engineers and munition workers. My boss at the insurance firm had offered me a position in a reserved occupation if I wished, but I was keen for a change and a more exciting life, so at seventeen and a half years of age I volunteered to join the Women's Royal Naval Service. At the same time I also signified that I was willing to serve abroad, for it had always been my ambition to travel and the WRNS offered me the opportunity.

Gerry wrote begging me not to join the services, particularly not to volunteer for overseas service. He wanted me to be around when he came home on leave. If I had to join up he suggested I joined the Land Army. Much as I enjoyed the country, I did not feel that I was sufficiently well-built to withstand the rigours of a Land Army girl's life which involved some very heavy and back-breaking forms of work, nor could I see that life on a farm would provide the excitement I craved. Luckily my parents agreed with me. Although they did not wish me to leave home they realised that at eighteen I would be compelled to do some form of war work and if not the Land Army or services, I would most probably be drafted into a factory to make munitions or machines. So of the available selections they approved my choice of the WRNS.

My brother Alan, who was now almost sixteen was due to finish his course at the nautical college of Sir John Cass and take an apprenticeship with a shipping line. Correspondence flowed to and fro until he was offered a position with Watts'

Shipping Company. I hoped that by joining the WRNS I might get to a port and be able to see both Gerry and Alan occasionally.

The war continued with both triumphs and setbacks in the Middle East until Rommel and his troops were driven out of North Africa; May 1943 brought victory for the Allied forces in Tunisia. Pressing their advantage, the Allies made landings in Sicily in July 1943 and two days later, on 12 July, the port of Syracuse was taken.

Not all operations went according to plan. Mistakes were made. The landings in Sicily were the first occasion on which glider operations were used. It was a complete disaster. The gliders used were American craft, nicknamed Wakkos, made of canvas over a metal frame and were towed by American planes. The plan was to land airborne troops to capture the bridge at Syracuse. There was a miscalculation. Most of the gliders landed in the sea several miles short of their intended destination. Due to their form of construction they did not float. Those who were able to get out in time were left floundering in the water. Those unable to escape sank with their crafts. Around two hundred men were lost. The operation had taken place at nine o'clock at night. Those fortunate enough to be kept afloat by their Mae West life jackets tried to keep together through the night hoping to be picked up by a friendly craft. One group was found and rescued by a Greek destroyer the following morning. They were dried off, fed and given fresh clothing before being taken to Algiers, in North Africa. Some Airborne troops did get to Sicily and on to Italy where they fought hard and well, living up to their name 'The Red Devils' given them by their German opponents in recognition of the red berets they wore as part of their uniform and indicating the tenacity of their actions.

On 25 July we heard over the radio that Benito Mussolini, the pompous, strutting dictator of Italy, had resigned. It was at first difficult to believe, but further news bulletins confirmed the fact. The good news continued. On 3 September Allied landings were made on the Italian mainland and things began to look a little brighter on that front although the enemy were

75

still well-settled in the rest of Europe. On 11 September we were told Italy had surrendered. One down and two to go!

The Russians were fighting heroically and holding the Axis powers on their front line waiting for the Allies to take off some of the pressure by an invasion of Europe. Since the bombing of Pearl Harbour in Hawaii, the Americans had made the Pacific War their priority and although they did not declare war on Germany and Italy, Hitler solved the situation for us by declaring war on the USA. Many United States' ships had already been sunk by U-boat action, and although the US government was friendly towards Britain and sympathetic to our plight to the extent of sending supplies of materials, arms and food, the majority of the population did not wish their country to become involved in the fighting. Many of the good-hearted people got together to send parcels of clothing and food to people in Britain. These little luxuries were gratefully received in a country where tins of ham had disappeared from the shelves and instead we were offered Spam, a meat-flavoured mix of ingredients, or snoek steaks which were in fact whale meat.

Years went by without sight of a banana and even dried fruit was rare. However, we never starved and most people were healthier than they had ever been before. When the weekly ration ran out or housewives were desperate for ideas, it was possible to buy a cheap but sustaining meal at one of the British Restaurants set up in church or village halls throughout the country.

In the dark days of the war, various organisations had been formed of volunteers like the WVS, Women's Voluntary Service, now known as the Women's Royal Voluntary Service, and the Citizen's Advice Bureaux, mostly intended to help those unfortunates who had been bombed out of their homes and to provide tea and refreshments to the fire-fighters and others at work clearing up the mess left by the bombers. They also provided refreshments for troops in transit and many other services to the community. There was a general sense of warmth towards one's neighbour and a feeling that we were all in this together. That is not to say that there were no miscreants. There are always with us those who are only concerned for themselves and we had the 'wide boys' and 'spivs' who ran black markets, also the profiteers who saw their chance to cash in on the shortages and difficulties of others. But on the whole people helped each other when a need arose.

6

In April 1944 my notice to report to the WRNS arrived. At the same time Alan received his notice to join a ship. We had about three weeks to make our arrangements and say our goodbyes. I wrote to Jim, still in hospital having fallen over yet again and broken his other leg, after taking an unofficial day's leave in the town with his friends from the ward, saying I would be unable to visit him any longer. I sent a quick note to all my other correspondents to inform them of the change, handed in my notice at work, sent goodbyes to those friends still around, said farewell to my singing teacher and the lessons I had so enjoyed and had a last get together with the GTC.

It was a wrench for my parents to have a son and daughter leave in the same week, especially as far as Alan was concerned as there was no knowing where he was going or when we should see him again as shipping movements were extremely 'hush hush'. It was actually eighteen months before he and I met up again.

As for me the first steps of my great desire for travel and excitement were to take me just four miles from home! To my great chagrin I received a letter instructing me to report to a training depot at Mill Hill, North London, not later than 3 p.m. on Wednesday 26 April 1944. Enclosed was a list of items of civilian clothing I should require as follows:

> 1 overcoat or raincoat
> 1 hat or scarf for use in wet weather
> 2 nightdresses or pairs of pyjamas
> 1 or 2 pairs of walking shoes (low heels essential)
> 1 pair of indoor shoes

the usual underclothing, stockings etc.
(marked please)
toilet requisites including sufficient soap
(and soap flakes if desired) or soap coupons
for fourteen days, also hair brush and tooth brush
2 pairs ankle socks
Sports equipment including shorts, slacks,
bathing suit and gym shoes SHOULD BE
    BROUGHT
for use in physical training
As during air-raids, it may be necessary to sleep
in shelters, the following articles are also
desirable:
1 rug or coloured blanket
1 dressing-gown
One suitcase only is permitted. . . .

and a final sentence to round off the information:

No food or drink should be brought or sent to
the training depot.

With suitcase in hand containing these personal pieces of equipment I made my farewells to my parents and Cindy, now a schoolgirl of eleven, then boarded the bus for Mill Hill. Excitement and probably a little apprehension at starting a new kind of life filled my heart and images of myself in a smart navy uniform at work in some busy port amongst ships of all kinds filled my mind. Although Wrens did not actually sail ships, there were a few who went out in boats to deliver mail and had harbour duties and even some who went on board ships to strip and clean some of the guns. I could just possibly be lucky enough to be chosen for such an active occupation.

I did not have long to speculate as the short journey soon brought me to the town of Mill Hill. There it was necessary to ask my way to the training depot. I discovered I needed to board another bus to take me to the top of a long hill on which the Depot, or HMS *Pembroke III* as it was called, stood. The bus

deposited me at the entrance of a large brick building with many windows and an imposing doorway in its centre. Wings of rooms stretched to the right, left and behind the central building. In front was a large open tarmac area on which stood a flag pole flying the Union Jack. Taking my courage and my suitcase in my hands, I walked across this wide and empty area and through the open front doorway. Inside women dressed in WRNS uniform and girls like myself in civilian dress were standing in the large, high-roofed hallway. A Wren petty officer took my reporting slip and other details before all new entrants were ushered into a spacious room containing a platform at one end. While we waited for the unknown next procedure, tentative 'hellos' were made and enquiries as to 'Where is your home?', 'Have you come far?' 'What made you choose the WRNS?' and a few nervous comments, 'I wonder what happens next' or 'What do we do now?'. This buzz of conversation was cut short by the arrival of a Wren officer upon the platform. In the quiet which followed she introduced another officer with several rings of gold braid around her sleeves as the commanding officer of the training depot. All listened attentively as we were welcomed and told a little about the WRNS and what would be expected of us as serving members. That was the first of the few times we ever saw our commanding officer. Her talk finished, we were handed over to another officer who explained some of the processes in becoming a fully fledged Wren, then we were again handed over to a petty officer who, using live models and picture illustrations, informed us of the hierarchy of the various ranks and insignias of the naval uniform and how they were to be addressed.

Eventually we were divided into groups and a Wren guide showed us to our 'cabins'. From this time on, every part of the building was referred to as if it were part of a ship. The kitchen became the galley; the dining-room, the mess; the room where we relaxed in off duty periods, the fo'c'sle; the large hall running through the centre of the building, main deck; and of course our bedrooms became our cabins. The cabins were shared by as many as eight Wrens, sometimes more depending on the size of the room. Double-decker metal bunks, each one covered with a blue and white counterpane on which a large white anchor was the central design, lined the walls. A small cupboard was allotted to each bed and in this all our belongings had to be stored or, in naval terms, stowed.

Being pretty agile I chose a top bunk where I would have an overall view of my room-mates and not risk hitting my head on the springs above me if I sat up suddenly. It was not until early next morning when we were all aroused by a loud 'Show a leg there!' and stepping out of bed still half-asleep, that I remembered the disadvantage of a top bunk and the long drop to the floor. I was not the only one to forget and there were a few wry grins from us and some sleepy chuckles from those on the lower stratum.

On entry we had been issued with a navy-blue overall dress of hard-wearing material which had coloured tabs denoting the division to which we were assigned. These were to be worn whenever we were on duty for the first two weeks of our probation. Those same two weeks were filled with duties,

HOUSE DUTY

" LESS NOISE DOWN THERE! "

squad drilling and lectures. Separated into divisions with suitable naval names, we were allocated various duties in the maintenance and running of the training establishment. Mess duties entailed cleaning, clearing and serving in the large hall or general mess in which we took our meals, or in the officers' mess; galley duties involved similar duties helping the cooks; house duties meant general cleaning in the rest of the building. I was detailed to this last section and with four or five others was roused at 5 a m We were then allowed to get a mug of tea from the galley before commencing our duties. My section was to clean the basement area. The first task given to myself and one other girl was to scrub a flight of stone steps. The petty officer provided a bucket, scrubbing brushes, soap and cloths and told us to get on with it. Luckily my companion shared my sense of humour and on hands and knees we set to work. We had a regular 'Gert and Daisy' act going which gave us great amusement and made the job more fun, when about halfway down the flight the face of the petty officer appeared above us and a voice commanded, 'Less noise down there!' Our giggles subsided and we completed our task as quietly as mice.

The steps finished, there were sinks to clean and brass taps to shine until it was time to break for breakfast. We had by then worked up a hearty appetite and were ready for anything the cooks dished up. After breakfast all divisions were mustered on the quarter-deck for roll-call and prayers, the quarter-deck being the large tarmac area in the front of the building containing the flag pole on which flew the Union Jack. This flag had to be saluted each time it was passed and naval discipline insured we did this by not allowing us to enter the building directly from the front gate, but instead we were commanded to walk a two thirds circle around the quadrangle, past the pole, before entering the doors.

It was at this muster that 'orders of the day' were given and defaulters named. In our third week of training my name was amongst them. This is how it was. For the first two weeks of our initiation we were confined to quarters, but on the third week as enrolled Wrens, naval discipline relented sufficiently to allow its recruits two hours' freedom each day when off-duty.

We were compelled to report back to the regulating office on the dot at the end of the two hours. I never suffered from home sickness, certainly not at Mill Hill for I was still on familiar territory, but I had made friends with some girls from the north of England and a few were missing their homes and families badly. It was too far for them to visit their homes, so I decided that the next best thing would be a visit to my home only four miles away. They were willing and keen so at the next opportunity, on a Sunday afternoon, shipshape and very much aware of our new serge uniforms, the four of us set off and made the bus ride to my family's house.

It was a lovely sunny spring day and we surprised my parents sitting in the garden by the cherry tree, just coming into its beautiful deep pink blossom. Once I had introduced my friends and explained our limited leave, my mother hurried to produce tea and cakes for us all. Away from the starkness and strict discipline of the training centre, enjoying the sunshine and softness of the spring garden, we were all able to relax and chat easily with my mother and father. In this way time passed quickly, too quickly, and I suddenly realised that if we were to get back within our two hour limit we had to be moving at once.

Quickly we made our goodbyes and went for the bus which we caught by the skin of our teeth. This took us as far as Mill Hill town where we arrived just in time to see the bus which was to take us up the long hill disappear from view. There was nothing else for us to do but walk. It was a long warm hike, which even with the fitness and vigour of youth took our breath away. Panting and red-faced we arrived at the regulating desk where the petty officer in charge took one look at our cards which had to be handed in every time we left the building, and snapped 'You are five minutes late'. I felt this to be unfair and after looking at my watch replied, 'I make it two minutes actually'. I should have kept quiet. Only that very morning our leading wren in charge had informed us that, 'We do not have defaulters in Howe Division'. We proved her wrong and the very next day our four names were called out on morning parade and we were compelled to step out from the ranks and march to join the line of defaulters who faced the rest of the assembled Wrens. We felt this to be an embarrassing and unfair indignity for the sake of a few minutes, but worse was to come. Once the parade had been dismissed, we defaulters were marched to the first officer's office and in our turn were ordered to salute and stand to attention while our crime was read out.

This was the only time I remember seeing the first officer at close hand. She appeared to us a smart, but unsmiling woman in her thirties sitting behind a heavy wooden desk. Her stern gaze remained on us while the charge was read out causing us to feel that we were once again naughty school children being reprimanded by the headmistress. This time I didn't argue. It was a great relief when after a short lecture on naval discipline we were let off with a warning and no loss of further two hour leave privilege. I still feel that if we had not had to march all round that wretched quarter-deck to salute the flag we would have been in on time.

Recruits to the WRNS came from many backgrounds and classes of society. Most of us accepted the tasks and restrictions of naval regime with good humour and a keeness to 'do our bit' for the war effort, but as volunteers we were free to leave at any time in those first two weeks if we felt so inclined. A few girls did. The opinion of those of us who stuck it out was disparaging towards those weaker of the weaker sex. 'Can't take it huh!' was the general thought as we squared our shoulders and pressed on.

We continued to get what fun we could out of our duties and a more enjoyable way of polishing main deck was to take turns sitting on the large thick dusters while your companion pulled you along the length of the deck. It had the advantage of producing a lovely shine in half the time, but only when the petty officer wasn't looking!

Not all recruits were as young as myself. A few older women also joined the service and went through the same training, many of them becoming non-commissioned or commissioned officers fairly quickly with their greater experience and qualifications, but the majority of us were seventeen to nineteen years of age and away from our families for the first time, our knowledge of the world, particularly sex, strictly limited.

85

Certainly, I knew very little of the so called 'facts of life'. The nearest my mother ever came to telling me was to say, 'Keep your legs crossed whenever you go out with a boy,' with no further enlightenment, which left me very puzzled indeed, so when the WRNS doctor gave a lecture illustrated by slides, it was all a great and even embarrassing revelation to me. I was very thankful for the darkened room to hide my blushes and when the lights went on again I could see I was not the only bashful girl. Our new knowledge caused a number of thoughtful countenances.

The two weeks, initial training continued with duties, lectures and more squad drill. At the end of this time came the kitting out process in preparation for our enrolment. Kitting-out was a further enlightening experience. Many girls had chosen to join the WRNS because, of the three women's services, the WRNS uniform was the most attractive. Its unbelted, double breasted navy jacket and straight skirt were more flattering to most girls' figures than the more bulky uniforms of the ATS and WAAF and the little round style hat was considered rather cute. The tricorn hats of the wren officers were even more dashing. Taken to the equipment store, each girl was issued with two jackets and two skirts. The problem here was to make sure that the dye of the jacket matched the dye of your skirt as there were slight variations which looked odd when put together. Once teamed up, the rest of the kitting was straightforward. We were issued with one hat, three shirts with separate collars, two ties, one greatcoat, one raincoat, two pairs of flat, black, lace-up shoes, a pullover, moneybelt and gloves. Our underwear, for which we had to pay out of a grant of forty-five shillings, consisted of three vests, three pairs of black lisle stockings and three pairs of large navy-blue bloomers with elasticated knicker legs, which brought gasps of horror from the new recruits and were promptly stowed at the bottom of one's kitbag, never to see the light of day. These bloomers were known as 'blackouts' throughout the service. To contain these items we were given a long kitbag with drawstring top and a small attaché case just large enough to hold sufficient items for a forty-eight hour's leave. We were allowed our own choice of pyjamas and dressing-gown.

The only item that gave me problems were the shoes. Members of our family, and I am one, have almost all been endowed with long narrow feet for which, even in civilian life in those days, it was extremely difficult to find well-fitting shoes. Most manufacturers did not deviate from what they called standard fittings and anyone unfortunate enough not to conform had to suffer ill-fitting shoes and corns. It caused my mother many long weary searches and tears of frustration on my part trying to find an attractive and suitable pair of shoes. I usually had to end up with a pair that would have looked more in keeping on an elderly aunt. Not only are my feet extra narrow, but they stopped growing at the manufacturer's size 6½. Now the navy's sizing was even more rigid: they had no half sizes and certainly no narrow fittings. So I ended up with two pairs of ugly black shoes which even when tightly laced fell off my feet and looked more like a pair of rowing boats! When marching and drilling it was only my thick black stockings and will power which held them in place.

We gradually became accustomed to our new uniforms and the stiffness of our bright white collars. Learning to tie a tie correctly took a little time. Those girls used to wearing a tie with school uniforms had the advantage and there were many willing to help those less adept. All hair had to be above the collar so those with long tresses had either to cut them or roll them up. Hence the wearing of a ribbon or band around the head over which the hair was rolled to keep it off the collar and face. In this way, when off-duty, girls could keep their curls.

Caps were to be worn at the correct angle, slightly towards the right-hand side of the head with the bow of the black capband strictly on the side's centre. As Wrens and sailors became more seasoned in the service and moved away from the more 'pukka' and highly disciplined areas, caps were seen to be worn at varying angles, frequently on the back of the head with 'tiddly' bow to the fore, 'tiddly' being the navy's terms for being smart in dress as seen by the ratings themselves; not necessarily so described by those in authority. A favourite trick of some naval ratings was to tie a threepenny piece inside the bow to make it stand out boldly. New male naval ratings also liked to fade the colour of their wide blue collars to a paler blue to simulate those of the long-serving seamen. These large collars could be a problem when trying to put on a greatcoat as unless held down they could become rucked up and creased. I well remember my mother's expression when one day she and I walked out from seeing a film into the cinema foyer and saw a sailor struggling into his greatcoat being frustrated by his collar. Seeing my Wren uniform he called out 'Hey Jenny, come and give me a hand will you?' I went over, and facing him, put my arms around him under his arms, and held down the corners of his collar while he shrugged himself into his coat. I was just able to catch the amazed look on my mother's face before the sailor, a complete stranger said 'Thanks' and left.

It was considered very 'tiddly' for male ratings to fold their bell bottoms in such a way so as to have seven horizontal creases in the legs to represent the Seven Seas I was told. It was also 'tiddly' to have extra long streamers to the front tapes of their tops. These black tapes were allowed to be replaced by white ones on the occasion of a wedding. However, none of the variations were to be seen in the strict environment of a naval training establishment.

Towards the end of our second week we were called for personal interviews with one of the wren officers. This was to assess our capabilities and decide our future categories. Apart from a grammar school education I had no particular qualifications and only my short experience in the insurance office to offer. I knew I did not wish to be a steward or a cook and hoped for something more glamorous and exciting. I came away from the interview none the wiser as to the outcome of my fate but was left to speculate on the possibilities.

At the end of our three weeks as fully-fledged, enrolled Wrens complete with identity discs on which were inscribed our name and number, we were given our new postings. I was to be posted to special duties at *Pembroke V*. Where or what it was I had no idea.

Saying goodbye to our companions of those uprooting three

weeks which had transposed numbers of individual and uncertain young women into confident disciplined members of His Majesty's Royal Navy was a time of mixed feelings. For three weeks, those who had shared cabins or work had become close companions and friends. Now we were to be split up and dispersed to different parts of the country into many different categories of work and were unlikely to meet again except for a rare chance. This called for some regrets. On the other hand there was the anticipation and excitement of the unknown yet to come, of new places and new friends we had yet to meet. We were called into different groups and ordered to climb into the naval transports awaiting us. This occasion was our first experience of packing and carrying naval kitbags which at first we found clumsy and difficult to manage; however, with practice we soon learnt to sling them on to our shoulders and carry them with ease if not grace.

From the back of the naval truck I glimpsed streets, buildings and as the traffic became heavier I realised that we were travelling further into the capital's built-up outskirts. When the truck came to a halt and we disembarked, we found our destination to be New College in the area of North London. This was a transit quarters where we were to stay until a regular posting was found for us. In the meantime we were given duties to keep us occupied. I was assigned to night-watch duty in the regulating office, my first experience of the topsy-turvy life of night workers. I did not enjoy it as it gave me little opportunity to get to know other girls there and I found trying to sleep in daytime difficult. We still shared cabins with a number of others, all of whom worked different hours, so night-watchers were frequently disturbed by the chatting and noise of those in the course of their daily duties.

During the period of the day when I was not sleeping I was usually on my own, so I took myself off to explore the surrounding district. A short bus ride brought me to Golders Green and Hampstead. Hampstead had open spaces which gave me a chance to get away from buildings and traffic and provided a touch of countryside with tree-shaded areas, ponds and grassy slopes. If I wanted some company there was a

ON THE
MOVE

forces' canteen where I could find something to eat and drink and sometimes, somebody willing to join me in a game of table-tennis. Tables for this game were available in most forces' canteens and I became reasonably adept at hitting this little white ball to and fro. My prowess can probably be attributed to the continued number of night-watch duties I was forced to do through my WRNS services. One service helped another!

The forces' canteens were run by many groups all of whom were volunteers. There were the large and famous ones in London's centre such as the Queensberry All-Services Club in the London Casino, Old Compton Street, where stars of stage and screen came to entertain and where well-known bands provided music for dancing. Others run by the Salvation Army, YMCA and YWCA (Young Men's Christian Association and Young Women's Christian Association), Toc H and many more organisations, down to those in small villages where the village hall was provided to give refreshment and relaxation to any member of the services feeling the need for a quiet chat or escape from camp or quarters. Here the ladies of the Women's Institute, Mothers' Guild and others dispensed tea and sympathy when required. The NAAFI canteens found on most large forces service stations were run by the Navy, Army and Air Force Institutes and those who worked in them wore uniform with the NAAFI badge and were paid for their services. This service continued after the war when they still supplied a large variety of goods and services to the men, women and families of British forces all over the world.

My stay in New College was of fairly short duration of which I was glad. An order arrived one day posting me to a new quarters. Once more with kitbag and attaché case I boarded the naval truck and with other girls was whisked off into the unknown. It proved to be a slightly longer journey this time and I had hopes that my destination might be the coast and a port where I could really feel I was a part of the Royal Navy. No such luck! After two hours or so travelling the truck stopped and the petty officer in charge called the names of some Wrens who were told to dismount and report to their new quarters.

This done, we were off once more continuing our journey for a few more miles before the truck halted again. This time my name was among those called and with about six others I clambered out of the truck taking my belongings with me. We appeared to be in the courtyard of a large country house. I could see trees and open fields and in the distance the glint of water. There was an absence of the noise of traffic: instead bird song and fresh country smells filled the air.

A new petty officer took charge and directed us to a long low building inside of which was one vast long room where we were allocated bunks, once more a top one for me. Altogether there must have been around forty bunks in this room. Adjoining the courtyard across from the main house, it had been the stables and then the garage of the estate, and was entered by large double doors which opened directly on to the bunks and allowed little privacy.

The process of settling in started with tentative questions asked of those few girls who were around. The first question being, 'Where are we?' With their answer, 'Wavendon House, Bedfordshire,' I knew my hopes of a port were dashed. The glimpse of water I had seen was nothing more than a small lake in part of the grounds of the house. It was disappointing, but, still, one never knew what might turn up. There was always something new to see and do. Our companions were friendly, helpfully guiding us through the routine of the day and explaining the lay-out of the building and grounds. At lunchtime the gong signalled that the cooks were ready to serve the meal and we joined the queue to the hatchway where large plates of meat and vegetables swimming in thick brown gravy were served to us. I made a mental note to get a word in quickly before the steward with the gravy jug swamped my next meal.

Our meals were eaten at the usual long tables in a large room whose windows overlooked the shrubbery grounds at the back of the house. The more attractive rooms and outlooks were of course the preserve of the officers and petty officers. Although many Wrens were quartered in this house they were never all there together due to the varying hours they worked, so we never felt overcrowded. If one wanted solitude there were the

92

spacious grounds providing plenty of peaceful areas in which to walk or sit; a small woodland with winding paths; beside the lake; in the open parkland or the lengthy drive. In the sunny days of Spring and Summer these were all pleasant places in which to relax. We in Wavendon House were more fortunate in this respect than our contemporaries and near neighbours stationed in Woburn House, the Duke of Bedford's family home. They had to run the gauntlet of meeting aggressive stags from the herd of deer that ran free in the grounds when they walked back down the long drive after an off-duty excursion, not a pleasant experience in the dark or semi-dark, particularly in the rutting season.

On arrival I was still unaware of the category or job I was intended for. It was later in the day when all new entrants were called together by a petty officer to assemble in the house to be addressed by a WRNS officer. This officer informed us that we were to work in a very important and highly secretive capacity in the nearby town of Bletchley. Transport would collect us next morning and take us to this establishment where we would be further informed. Our curiosity was aroused, but we could discover nothing more and had to be content to wait. Accordingly, next morning we boarded a naval bus along with other girls going on duty and were transported through the countryside to the outskirts of the town of Bletchley. The bus came to a halt outside some large metal gates. Here an armed guard boarded the bus and examined pass cards produced by the passengers. Those of us without pass cards were ushered off the bus and into the lodge building beside the gates where we were detained until collected by a Wren officer.

In a quiet room, subdued and somewhat overwhelmed by the atmosphere of tight-lipped security around us, we were once more addressed by an officer who stressed the fact that our backgrounds had been closely investigated, particularly that of one of the girls whose father was of foreign extraction, and that we had all been cleared and considered suitable for work of such an extremely secretive nature. We were then asked to sign a document and told if we were to divulge any information gained about our work we would be liable to imprisonment.

This done we were then handed over in to the capable hands of a PO (petty officer).

I am glad to say that after a period of forty years, this bond of secrecy no longer binds, as there have been several books written about the work done at Bletchley Park, one of which is *Ultra Goes to War* by Ronald Lewin, but in 1944 and while hostilities continued we took our work and vows of secrecy in deadly earnest.

The grounds of the establishment were extensive. Long low prefabricated buildings covered much of the area. The main house appeared to be Victorian in style and rather over-fussily endowed with decoration on its exterior with many un-necessary bits and pieces, particularly so in those days of austerity. A brick-edged lawn with central flower borders lay before the main house and was surrounded by a tarmac drive. Our duties were carried out in the humbler regions of one of the prefabricated buildings known as Hut 8 and the only time I remember going to the house was on an occasion when my pocket was picked while I was in the ladies' room and my identity card, pass card and a £1 note were stolen. A cleaner discovered my identity card stuffed behind the WC, but the £1 note and pass card were never found. Losing a pass card was a serious business and of course I had to report it at once. This involved walking to the main house and being questioned by a civilian lady. For the following two weeks I had to leave the bus at the main gates and wait in the lodge until someone from my department came to identify me. I was then allowed to return with them to my work. After two weeks a fine of two shillings and six pence was imposed and I was issued with a new pass. This added insult to injury as we were only paid fourteen shillings a week when pay parade was held, so the loss of two and six pence made quite a hole in my pocket.

Station X, as Bletchley Park was called, was a combined operation. Army, Navy, RAF and civilians all worked there, though usually in separate departments. Secrecy was rife and in all the time I was there I never asked or learned what the people in the next room were doing. Station X was of course a station where enemy signals were intercepted and decoded by the brilliant brains of university professors and others in the intelligence service. It was only when a message needed to be collected or delivered that we met these lofty individuals and I doubt if they ever distinguished one Wren from another.

At the end of our corridor were the large teleprinter machines and their operators through which messages were relayed. The rattle of these machines accompanied us throughout our watch and at times we were called to collect some urgent signal needing immediate attention.

The senior duty officer of the watch was a naval officer supported by a Wren officer. The officers were changed quite frequently, the Wren officer in charge keeping strict discipline. When spoken to we were always referred to by our surname preceded by our rank, for example: Wren Jones or Leading Wren Smith. On one occasion a new naval officer arrived. The young lieutenant, not yet used to the rather stiff procedure, called across to me for a particular card. In doing so he used my Christian name. This caused a sudden silence throughout the room and I felt rather than saw our Wren officer's disapproval. I found the card, handing it to him without comment, but I believe he must have been reprimanded by the Wren officer as he always addressed us very formally from then on. The only time there was any relaxation was on night-watch when no Wren officers were present. Donald was a naval officer who was frequently in charge of our watch at night and was a pleasant bespectacled chap who was liked by us all. When he had a problem to solve he paced up and down the width of the room with furrowed brow and hands clasped behind him. Until the pacing stopped we did not interrupt or speak, but once he had resolved his problem and sat down, all relaxed once more.

In each watch there were four or five Wrens with a leading Wren as head of watch. Time was divided into three different watches; day-watch from 8 am–4 pm; evening-watch from 4 pm–midnight and night-watch from midnight–8 am. Each watch had an hour's break in which to take a meal in the naval canteen. We worked a week on each watch. The most tiring times were when we had what was called the short change over from day to night-watch. This meant coming off watch at 4 pm and returning to another eight hour watch at midnight. There was just time to get a meal and a few hour's sleep, but no time at all for recreation. We occasionally had a twenty-four or forty-eight hour leave which gave us a chance to put work and quarters behind us and breathe a different air for a while. It was not always possible to get home on these short leaves, as for a period of several months we were confined to a twenty mile radius of our work.

Means of travel were varied. On longer leaves we were given railway warrants to travel by train. Bletchley station was a railway junction with trains going to many areas, but all trains were overcrowded, did not always run on time and sometimes were diverted for other purposes. On one journey the train guard took pity on me when in a very overcrowded train he found me standing in the corridor. He kindly directed me to a spare seat in a first-class compartment although my warrant only entitled me to third-class seating. I had just come straight from a week's spell of night duty, so was probably looking a bit tired and wan and I was certainly glad to have a seat.

The government tried to persuade people not to travel by putting out posters saying 'Is your journey really necessary?' the antithesis to the posters advertising British Rail in this present age when customers are courted. Another hazard to travelling was that all station names and signpost directions had been removed. Even delivery vans had the firms' addresses painted out. This was in order to make it difficult for any invading enemy to find his way around. It also made it difficult for the inhabitants of Britain, unless familiar with that particular area. A good sense of direction was a godsend. Since other posters exhorting one to 'Keep Mum' and 'Careless Talk Costs Lives' were freely distributed on walls and hoardings everywhere, a stranger asking questions could easily look suspicious and be treated as suspect. In the days after the occupation of Holland, Belgium and France the people of Britain quite expected to find enemy parachute troops being dropped by air to back up any invading force across the Channel and watched out for possible spies. By 1944 we were fighting back in good heart, but were still mindful of keeping information from the enemy, and pill-box gun emplacements were ready for instant occupation should the need arise.

A number of American troops were stationed around our area of Bletchley and Wrens were invited to their dances. In return they were invited to dances held at our quarters. This was my first close contact with members of the USA and I found their approach a little unexpected and not always agreeable. To put it bluntly, they were not backward in coming forward; much too forward! After the first few encounters we girls learnt to deal with arising situations and once we had sorted out our varying forms of English language, got along quite well. Girls who 'dated', in American terms, or went out with American servicemen, were surprised and of course delighted to find that their escorts usually arrived with a small gift: a bar of chocolate; a packet of sweets or 'candy' or some other small surprise bought from their canteen; and in one case I remember, a bar of soap. Few girls were used to such courtesies from their British boyfriends. British servicemen were at a disadvantage in being paid much less than their American counterparts, but even taking this fact into consideration, it was generally not their custom to give gifts on taking out a girlfriend. Such attentions were usually reserved for birthdays and other special occasions.

The dances at the American bases were popular mostly for the wonderful food served at their buffet tables. After five years of food rationing to see these mouth-watering delicacies so lavishly provided set us all drooling! We were prepared to be polite and even try to jive or jitterbug in order to partake of such a feast.

As a dance, I at first found the jive unattractive. Those jiving used too much floor space and were a distinct hazard to others dancing on the floor. My initiation came at one of the American forces dances, when a stocky and ebullient young GI approached me with the words 'Can you jive?'

When I truthfully answered, 'No', he grabbed my hand and said, 'That's okay, I'll teach you'.

Before more could be said, I found myself hauled onto the dance floor, my protests unheard in the blare of the band. I was flung out, pulled back, twirled, twisted, and jigged, while my partner contorted his torso and legs in fantastic wriggles to the vibrant rhythm of the music. At the end of the dance I staggered, crumpled, red-faced and giddy into the supporting arms of my giggling girlfriends. They could laugh. Their turn was to come! In time, although maybe not excellent exponents, we at least became adept enough to follow our partners' steps in this infectious and energetic dance.

The American forces were also most helpful in providing lifts when we were hitch-hiking. Transport was hard to come by in our out of the way places, with few bus services. On the occasions when we had a day off duty and wanted a change of scene, our only chance of getting anywhere was by walking about one and a half miles into the village of Woburn Sands and trying to hitch a ride or, failing that, walk to the nearest main road in the hope of getting a lift on some transport going in our direction. I never tried hitch-hiking on my own, but always went with at least one other girl. In this fashion we travelled in lorries, forces' trucks, cars and jeeps. One lady motorist who was kind enough to shift all her luggage in order to make room for us, was driving a rather battered car which had no cap to its radiator. She made do with a piece of rag stuffed into the opening instead. We proceeded along the highway through a curtain of rising steam, stopping constantly to refill the radiator with water. Grateful as we were for the lift we were happy to say goodbye on reaching the point where our ways diverged.

When it came to getting a lift with an army convoy it was the practice of the last truck in the convoy to stop and pick up service personnel pedestrians. If the truck happened to contain servicemen we found a number of willing hands eager to heave us up over the high back boards of the truck. It often meant we were subjected to plenty of banter from the male occupants, but it was always good-humoured and we learnt to give as good as we got.

Returning from a short forty-eight hour leave one day, my friend Barbara and I were picked up just outside St Albans by two GI's in a jeep. It was our first experience of this mode of

HITCH HIKING IN A JEEP

transport. We soon found it had its disadvantages. We had to literally hang on to our hats and were for once glad of our tight skirts as we tore along the old Roman road of Watling Street which leads towards the Welsh border. Our driver and his friend were protected by their windscreen, but Barbara and I received the full force of the strong blast caused by our fast and furious dash along the highway. With chinstraps down, hair flying and holding on to our dignity and whatever part of the vehicle happened to be handy, we arrived in Fenny Stratford in record time. Breathless and dishevelled we thanked the GI's for their help before they zoomed off into the distance, leaving us to restore some order to our appearance before returning to duty. By these various methods I was able to visit Bedford, Aylesbury, St Albans and one or two other places in our area.

When managing to get to London on a short leave, it was sometimes possible to get free tickets for one of the current shows. Spare tickets were made available for members of the services on leave in London through Forces' information centres in the capital. Popular shows in those days were the romantic musicals. On one of my longer leaves I took my mother to see Ivor Novello's *The Dancing Years*, a charming musical full of romance and wonderful melodies which took our minds far from the drab, harsh reality of life outside the theatre doors and for a short while absorbed our thoughts with a delightful fantasy of a kinder, more beautiful world.

Soon after the outbreak of war many of the beautiful and famous pictures and other art treasures of the country had been removed from London and put into 'mothballs' or, in other words, safe storage. Instead of going to the National Gallery to see the paintings, one went instead to hear Myra Hess, the pianist give her lunch-time concerts. Concerts were given by other musicians in churches or any suitable buildings through-out the years of the war. These were often entirely free and no tickets required. Music was found to be a great restorative for the soul. One piece of music in particular had a special significance for the people of Britain and those in the occupied countries who continued to resist the common enemy. It was Beethoven's Fifth Symphony which opens with four notes, three short and one long, which translated into the Morse code gives the letter V, V for Victory. This was used as the call sign for the BBC's broadcasts to Europe and although the rest of the symphony may have been a mystery to many, the first four notes were familiar and meaningful to all.

Noel Coward's song 'London Pride' gave new heart to the people of that city when they were undergoing the dreadful days and nights of the Blitz. Many other songs composed in those days had special meanings to those families parted by the conflict, some had the yearning qualities of looking forward to happier times such as 'When the Lights Come On Again All Over the World' or 'There'll be Bluebirds Over the White Cliffs of Dover'. Vera Lynn, known as 'The Forces Sweetheart' did a great job with her singing of these popular songs, touching a cord in most people's hearts. Among the songs popular to march to were 'Roll out the Barrel', 'Kiss me goodnight Sergeant Major', a cynical view of the army life of a Private, 'I've Got a Lovely Bunch of Coconuts', and a song the British Expeditionary Force (BEF) had so confidently, and as it turned out, over optimistically sung on their way to France, 'We're Going to Hang out the Washing on the Seigfried Line. Have You Any Dirty Washing Mother Dear?' perhaps not so easy to march to, but still popular:

'Bless 'em all, bless 'em all
The long and the short and the tall.
Bless all the sergeants and WOI's. . . .'

There are of course many more which were popular at the time and with the arrival of the American Forces in 1942 came a new wave of songs from the other side of the Atlantic.

Jean Metcalfe kept families in touch with their loved ones overseas in combat areas through relaying messages and music with her friendly voice over the radio waves. After the war in 1948, when troops were still sorting out the aftermath of hostilities, her opposite number broadcasting from the forces' side was Cliff Michelmore. Listeners were delighted when a romance blossomed over the air waves and Jean and Cliff were married. Cliff Michelmore served in the Royal Air Force with the Air Ministry and Bomber Command HQ during the war years. Other entertainment was provided by ENSA the Entertainments National Service Association who put on shows for troops at home and abroad. I had had thoughts of joining ENSA and even went as far as arranging a date for audition.

Just before I was due to go, I met by chance a man who was a driver for ENSA. He overheard me discussing the coming audition with a girlfriend while we were having coffee in the canteen of the film studios and seriously advised me not to join. He probably believed me to be too young and innocent to stand the hazards of such a life. His comments, along with my parents' disapproval had their effect. I reconsidered my action and on reaching London I rejected the audition and went to the ballet instead.

Many famous stars of theatre and films went to areas where troops were in action to bring a welcome touch of laughter and glamour into their lives for a brief while, Gracie Fields and Bob Hope among them. There were also those stars and comedians such as Norman Wisdom and Frankie Howerd who started in the entertainment business with ENSA or camp shows and made their names known to a wider audience when peace came. Many ENSA shows provided excellent entertainment, but not all. It was a joke going around amongst the services that at some ENSA shows the troops had to be locked in to the hall to be sure of providing an audience!

Before the war Henry Hall and his band had been one of the most popular orchestras on the radio. They always ended their performance with a signature tune with the following words:

> 'Here's to the next time and our merry meeting.
> Here's to the next time, we send you all our greetings.
> Put it to music, sing it to rhyme,
> Now all together, here's to next time.'

They were the BBC dance band for many years.

With the advent of the American forces, British listeners and audiences were introduced to a new musical sound, that of Glen Miller and his orchestra. His melodious and catchy arrangements of songs and tunes were played everywhere. A great favourite was one called 'In the Mood' which even my father, whose preference was for classical chamber music, liked. Glen Miller's mysterious disappearance on a flight to Paris soon after the liberation of that city was a shock to everyone and a great loss to his admirers.

A radio programme which started during the war was 'The Brains Trust' in which a panel of experts discussed and answered questions. In answering, Professor Joad nearly always used the phrase 'It all depends. . . .' This caught on with the general public as a popular catch-phrase and made him a well-known radio personality. 'The Brains Trust' was one of my father's favourite programmes and must have been popular with many other people as it lasted a great number of years.

'Band Wagon' a radio show with Richard Murdoch and Arthur Askey which purported to take place on the roof of Broadcasting House was extremely popular. Arthur Askey's 'Hello playmates' became another catch-phrase. Cyril Fletcher, who was an 'old boy' of my brother's school in Barnet, kept radio listeners amused with his rather naughty 'Odd Odes'. I am not sure if the headmaster would have approved of some of them. It was during the war years that radio announcers became personalised by introducing themselves before reading the news i.e. 'This is the nine o'clock news and this is Alvar Liddell reading it.' Up until then they had wafted through the radio air waves as unknown, disembodied voices.

Another voice we grew to recognise was that of Charles Hill the radio doctor whose deep bumbling voice accompanied our cornflakes or porridge every morning with his homilies on health. Sometimes we tuned in our radios to hear the nasal and objectional voice of 'Lord Haw-Haw' or William Joyce, broadcasting his daily disinformation and propaganda from Germany. All BBC broadcasting closed down at 10.45 p m when the announcer wished all listeners 'Goodnight' and the National Anthem was played.

In the film world the comedian George Formby made us smile with his portrayals of a shy, unsophisticated young man and his singing and playing of his ukelele. I once bumped into him turning a corner in one of my mad dashes down the studio corridor, causing him to drop the articles he was carrying. He did not look too happy then! Many of the films of the time came from America giving rather glamourised ideas of going to war. Their film of *Mrs Miniver* starring Greer Garson and Walter Pidgeon, a story set in England, gave an unrealistic version of a family in wartime conditions, but we enjoyed the films anyway.

In 1943 the film *Casablanca* starring Ingrid Bergman and Humphrey Bogart was a great success due in part I think to the song 'As Time Goes By', which caught on and was sung and played everywhere. *This is the Army* was another musical film giving an American version of army life. Lupino Lane starred in *Me and My Girl* in 1943, a show enjoying a current revival and which introduced the song and dance called 'The Lambeth Walk' popular in all the dance halls at that time. The film that made Judy Garland famous and took us far away from the dark days of war into a world of wonderful, colourful fantasy was of course *The Wizard of Oz*. We loved it then as it is still loved now. In the more serious films, Leslie Howard was a great actor appearing in films such as *Gone With the Wind*, *The Scarlet Pimpernel*, *Pimpernel Smith* and *First of the Few* in which he played the part of R J Mitchell, the designer of the Spitfire plane. Sadly Leslie Howard lost his life when he was returning to London from Lisbon, Portugal, a neutral country and a German Luftwaffe crew shot down the civilian aeroplane in which he was flying.

London was full of men and women in uniforms, many strange foreign uniforms among them, some colourful enough to star in musical comedy. Gold braid abounded and it was difficult to work out who you should or should not salute, so we did our best to ignore it.

7

My work at Bletchley Park proved to be extremely interesting although not actively exciting. I was mainly concerned with the indexing of signals intercepted from U-boats and among the messages of hostile action with regard to ships sighted and attacked were often those of a more humane and personal nature, such as informing the captain of the U-boat of the birth of a son or daughter. Other naval manoeuvres of ships, ours as well as the enemy's, were plotted and followed, and on one occasion I was able to watch the passage of my brother's ship in a convoy through the Mediterranean Sea. Such convoys suffered continual air strike attacks from enemy aircraft based in France and Italy, and when I was chatting with Alan one day, I asked what it felt like to be under fire in such conditions. He, a sixteen-year-old apprentice when these actions took place, replied that the apprentices were kept so busy carrying the ammunition to the guns on board, that they had no time to feel anything; and changed the subject.

When a U-boat was captured and brought into a London dock, Wrens from our section were given permission to go aboard to view it. I was amazed at the confined quarters in which the crews lived and worked. Each section of the vessel was separated by thick metal bulwarks in which a circular hatch standing about two feet above the deck was the only means of passing from one section to another. With our straight-cut uniforms it was necessary for we Wrens to hitch our skirts rather high in order to get our legs over and through to the next section. This we did as modestly as was possible, but were unable to avoid exposing a fair amount of leg, only to bob up the other side and find the grinning face of a British naval rating waiting for us. We had similar problems in descending the metal ladder from the conning tower. A member of the British Navy was standing by the base of the ladder to help?!

Apart from these incidents we found the visit extremely interesting, particularly as we were also able to see the Schnörkel attachment which enabled the U-boats to remain submerged for long periods of time and which had caused some puzzlement to our naval intelligence section before we discovered the reason. Seeing the torpedo section, from where the weapons which caused so much destruction were fired, brought to mind the importance of the work we did.

In early June 1944 there was an atmosphere of subdued excitement and tenseness at Station X. On 6 June the Allied forces made landings on the beaches in Normandy. The second front had begun. The Russians had for some time been calling to the Allied command to start another offensive to relieve the pressure they were receiving from the Axis forces and on 6 June D-day, their request was fulfilled. Thousands of Allied troops were conveyed across the Channel in flat-bottomed landing craft and in the early hours of the morning established themselves on the soil of France once more. Hitler's forces were surprised, but put up a strong resistance. Our work at Bletchley Park was trebled as signals flashed frantically to and fro. I was on night-watch at the time and at the end of the first week I went home on a forty-eight hours' leave and slept solidly for the first sixteen hours of it, without even waiting to have a meal. My mother asked no questions, but just left me to sleep it out.

Not long before D-day I had received a short letter from my pen-friend Jack saying he was back from the Middle East, in England and hoped we would get a chance to meet. It was the last letter I received from him. A few weeks after the Normandy landings all my letters were returned marked 'Hospital address unknown'. Sadly he must have been one of the casualties of the offensive. Of my other correspondents, Ken was still on the Italian front and Gerry in the Orkneys. For most of that summer I was quartered in Wavendon House and on some of my occasional hours off duty I helped the Wren gardener with

106

a little weeding in the grounds. Working in a garden has always been a pleasure to me. I find it has great therapeutic value when one is troubled in any way.

Woburn Sands was a small and quiet village within some pretty countryside. The people of the village had turned their local hall into a canteen for members of the forces. It sported the usual table-tennis and provided tea and buns. Barbara and I made our way here on off-duty periods during the day. Sometimes we were challenged to a game of table-tennis by soldiers or airmen from the area who also wandered in, but it was not a busy canteen, rarely more than half a dozen people were in there at a time as I remember.

There were some lovely walks around the village which were even more beautiful when the heather was in bloom. Barbara and I had been walking, gathering armfuls of these purple blooms to brighten up our cabin, when we met Max, a young Danish man we knew who was then in the Pioneer Corps stationed in the area. Max insisted on carrying our bunches of heather back to our quarters for us in spite of our protests. He showed no embarrassment at being seen walking through the village in uniform holding the mass of flowers. In the 1940s an Englishman would probably have flushed a vivid scarlet to be seen in such circumstances. He would have considered it to be an affront to his masculinity. Now, in the 1990s I do not suppose it would worry our young men to any extent as views and customs have changed so much over the last forty years.

Towards the end of summer most of the girls sleeping in the garage were moved to other quarters, Barbara and I among them. Some of us were transferred to Stockgrove Park, a large mansion house in beautiful grounds, situated on a hill just outside Leighton Buzzard. The move was from the ridiculous to the sublime. With six other girls, Barbara and I shared a beautiful cabin, or bedroom, with large windows and a magnificent view, on the first floor of this luxuriously designed house. There were polished parquet floors at our feet, several marvellous bathrooms containing all the up-to-date plumbing accoutrements and soft cork tile flooring and at the foot of the wide staircase, its polished balustrades enclosed and protected by board panels for the duration of war, was a large recreational area holding a table-tennis table. All rooms had large windows and light permeated everywhere. Such a contrast to our previous garage quarters.

There was only one drawback to this perfect place: it was four miles to the nearest town for shops or entertainment and the only way to get there was on foot. Unless one had a 'late pass' one was obliged to be back in quarters by 10 p.m. Consequently the whole of the time I was stationed there I never saw the finish of any of the films showing at the local cinema. It was necessary to leave by 9 o'clock to allow one hour for our walk back if we were to report at regulating office on time. Occasionally we were given a lift by a local farmer or lorry driver and sometimes an RAF vehicle going our way, but more often it was 'Shanks' pony' which no doubt helped to keep us fit.

A short cut to the main road passed through a field where men in unfamiliar grey uniforms worked, helping the farmer in the harvesting of potatoes. We discovered them to be German prisoners of war. It seemed odd that some of the enemy we had been fighting should be so close to our back door and that they should look just like any other young men. Remember that up until the outbreak of war, to see a man who was not a British man was a rarity to young people from quiet backgrounds such as mine. Hitler's propaganda and the news films we had seen had encouraged the belief that all German youth were large, blond, goose-stepping and aggressive members of a self-styled master race.

Leighton Buzzard as I knew it was a small country town in which the most notable building was probably the corn exchange. The town was large enough to boast a Woolworth's store, a cinema, several pubs, an hotel and a number of small shops. The local community had also provided a forces' canteen where we could relax with a cup of tea, chat or play table-tennis. They also ran the occasional dance where we could meet young men of the various services stationed nearby or home on leave. It made a pleasant change to meet up with members of the opposite sex, for living in a Wrens' quarters was rather like an all girls' school where seeing a male was a rare event. Although we found plenty of partners to dance with, their interest diminished when they discovered that to see us safely home meant a four mile walk; eight miles if they had to return to town!

One day I went in to Leighton Buzzard and was challenged to a game of table-tennis by a sailor I met in the canteen. It was unusual to find a male member of the Royal Navy in this country town far from port. He was, he told me, home on leave from Portsmouth and feeling a bit lonely as none of his friends were home at the same time. He suggested we spent the evening together. I said I was sorry, but it was not possible and explained my problem on getting back to quarters.

'If I can get you transport, will you stay?' he asked. With this proviso I agreed. 'Right, come with me,' said Ben. We walked through the town and to my surprise stopped outside the police station, 'Wait here' I was told and Ben disappeared over the wall.

I was beginning to get a little concerned about what he was up to, when he reappeared grinning.

'That's okay then,' he said 'Come on.'

My worries were unfounded, his actions were all perfectly legal. It turned out that his father was the local police inspector and that the family lived in the house attached to the police station. His father had very kindly agreed to make sure I was delivered back to my quarters on time by the police car! That was the beginning of my friendship with the King family.

As things turned out I became more friendly with the family than I did with Ben. On the rare occasions I saw him on leave, our meetings turned out to be a series of verbal sparring matches. Mrs King was a lady of commendable patience who was tragically paralysed in all her limbs and was only able to move her head. She retained her speech, but was economic in its use. Her daughter, Beryl, then sixteen years of age, helped to care for her mother with the aid of a friend of the family who called several times a day. The house being attached to the police station meant that Inspector King was able to be on hand much of the time. The wheelchair was placed in such a

109

POTHOLE IN THE BLACKOUT

way that Mrs King had a view of passers-by on the road through the tall Victorian sashed window, but there seemed to be few other diversions she was able to enjoy. On some of my off-duty hours I called in for a chat and a cup of tea. On Christmas Day, coming off a duty-watch, I was invited to join the family and found they had saved a huge Christmas dinner for me, complete with a large glass of cider. I appreciated the gesture and the fact that they had sacrificed some of their rations for my benefit.

At my request my parents had sent my bicycle to Stockgrove Park and this enabled me to travel more freely in the local area. One winter evening I was invited by the inspector and Beryl to join them at a dance in the nearby village of Wing. After finishing duty-watch and having had my evening meal, I set off to cycle the four miles to Leighton Buzzard. It was a pitch-black night, not a hint of moon or stars to help light my way. The long drive was overshadowed by trees and the feeble rays of my cycle lamp, dimmed to comply with blackout regulations, did little to guide me. As I sped as fast as I dared towards the end of the drive, the front wheel suddenly jolted and collapsed beneath me. I was flung to the ground, my bicycle in a heap beside me. When after a few seconds my breath returned, I gingerly picked myself up and was relieved to find I had suffered nothing more than a few bruises, thanks largely to the thickness of my greatcoat, but due to the extreme darkness I was unable to see how much damage had been done to my bicycle. Feeling around with my hands I realised I had cycled straight into one of the large potholes which dotted the drive, unrepaired through the five years of war. I found the handlebars of my bicycle luckily still attached to the rest of the machine, also my lamp. This had suffered a broken bulb and no longer emitted even the feeblest of rays, but I reckoned it would not make that much difference. I decided to remount and continue to Leighton Buzzard. It was a somewhat erratic journey as I found great difficulty in steering, but perseverance paid off and I finally reached the Kings' house. Inspector King and Beryl were all ready and waiting to go and were wondering what had happened to delay me. When I explained the circumstances the inspector said he would drive me back to quarters after the dance and examine my bicycle in the morning.

It was not until the following day when I was able to return and take a good look at my machine in daylight, that I realised the extent of the damage. The front wheel was completely twisted, looking more like a slice of convoluted lemon than a circular radial wheel. The inspector was amazed that I had managed to cycle the four miles with it in such a condition: the brakes did not work too well either. However, he very kindly said he would have it repaired for me and I could pick it up in a few days' time.

After five years of war, most young people over the age of eighteen were serving in one of the armed forces and so uniform was the general dress of the day. It was interesting to watch the young men's reactions to the monotony of such garments at the dance halls. The dance at Wing was in an RAF area and so air force blue was the predominant colour among both male and female dancers. However, there were a few girls in khaki ATS uniform. When dancing began, the first to be claimed as partners were the civilian girls in their colourful dresses. I being the only Wren there was the next to be asked, and then the ATS and WAAF's began to find partners. It seemed to be an instinctive reaction on the males' part to break away from the monotony and uniformity of their everyday existence.

When men were in short supply at some dances, women danced together, as all dancing was ballroom dancing, apart from the jitterbugging or jive introduced by the American servicemen, and even that required a partner. The Paul Jones was a dance which gave those who came without a partner a chance to find one. In this dance girls joined hands and made a circle facing another circle made by the men. To the strains of a lively and particular tune, the circles rotated in opposite directions. When the music stopped, the person who stood opposite you was your partner for the next dance. When the dance finished the circles were reformed and the whole thing was repeated. Among the waltzes, quickstep and slow foxtrots there was usually an old-time selection of dances such as the

Valeta, St Bernards and the Gay Gordons, the last of which was a sure way of livening up the evening as the men spun and twirled their partners until they were dizzy and needed the male supporting arm to be escorted from the floor. At some dances novelty dances such as the Palais Glide, and Lambeth Walk would be included also a South American medley such as the tango, rumba and mamba. You would always be guaranteed plenty of space when dancing these as many of the men fought shy of them.

The floor was usually crowded for the elimination dances when there was a chance of gaining a prize. In these the music stopped abruptly and everyone stood still. The MC (master of ceremonies) then requested those wearing a certain colour or standing in a certain section of the room to leave the floor. When they had done so, the music began again. Each time the music stopped the MC made a further stipulation and more couples left until finally only one couple remained on the floor. The lucky couple were then each presented with a prize.

The enjoyable thing about the dances then was that you danced to the music of live musicians, not a disc jockey's records or tapes. If you were not dancing you had the alternative opportunity of watching the band manipulate their instruments and listening to the MC's comments; also the music was never so loud as to prevent a chat with your friends. It was a pleasant, friendly and sociable way of spending an evening together.

The accepted way to find a partner if going without an escort, was for the girls to wait, sitting or standing around the dance floor until a man came up to them and asked, 'May I have this dance?' It was politeness on the girl's part to accept. They would then stay together for a group of three dances before the band played a long chord. This was the signal to return to your seats to which the man escorted you before saying, 'Thank you' and rejoining his friends. Should he decide he was attracted to you and you reciprocated the feeling, he might stay with you for the rest of the evening. The signal that the dance was coming to an end was the announcement of the 'Last Waltz'. The man who partnered a girl in the last waltz usually asked to see her home and often this led to other meetings being arranged. Many girls met their future husbands at such an occasion.

8

Down to the Sea in Ships

Tell me, tell me, little Wren, do you sail the sea?
Oh no, I sit at home all day upon the captain's knee.
Have you smelled the ozone or the odour of the tar?
The only smell that I know, is the smell of NAFFI
    char.
But surely you have felt the sting of salt upon the air?
Well no, but I've been tickled by my woollen
    underwear.
And what about your stockings – it is true they're
    fully-fashioned?
All information of that sort is very strictly rationed.
Perhaps your job is secret. Tell me, do you work in
    code?
Depends on what you mean by work, to quote
    Professor Joad.
D'you sleep in just a hammock, or in a wooden bunk?
I slept in issue nighties until the darned things
    shrunk.
Have you a man in every port as sailors always
    boast?
I haven't men in any, – but I've officers in most!

(*A ditty composed by an anonymous author which did the round of our
WRNS quarters.*)

The work and rest routine continued at Bletchley Park and
Stockgrove Park broken only by the occasional leave or forty-
eight hour pass. Most of the Wrens regretted being so far

distant from the sea and the activity of the ports. One day a friend and I decided to do something about it. We both had a forty-eight hour leave due and on the spur of the moment decided to use it on a visit to Folkstone. I had been born there, but as we had moved away when I was three I had few memories of how it looked. My mother was still in contact with friends there and it would be a chance to say hello. Collecting our passes and travel warrants, Jessie and I set out.

Arriving in Folkestone we found accommodation in a Salvation Army hostel on The Leas, the cliffs overlooking the sea. It was wonderful to walk out of the door and have the English Channel at our feet. Just to see the sea glinting and gleaming in the spring sunshine, listen to the gentle swishing of its eddies on the shingle and to smell and feel the salt tang of the air around us was pure delight. Our morning was spent walking along the cliffs, exploring the town, which had suffered heavy bombing and shelling from the guns sited on the French coast. During the periods of each day when the shelling commenced, many inhabitants of the town had taken their families to shelter in the deep caves which studded the white chalk cliffs around the town or into the Kent country-side out of range of the guns. When the guns grew quiet the people returned to assess the damage done and take up as normal a life as was possible in the circumstances. One friend, who was a child of about eight years old at this time, remembers being put in the dark recesses of the coal cellar by her mother when the shelling started. This was considered the safest spot in the house. She will never forget the blackness or the smell of coal.

When we had finished our exploration of the town Jessie and I called on my parents' friends. As they had not seen me since the age of three, a strange Wren of eighteen years knocking on their door was quite a surprise to them, but they gave Jessie and me a great welcome and called in other friends who had known me as a baby. Although I could not remember the incidents they recounted, between them they had a great time reminiscing. I was able to bring them up to date with family news and had a few photographs of my brother who was only one year old when they had last seen him. At lunchtime we said our goodbyes, our final ones as it happened, as I was never to see them again for about a year later our friend died.

After lunch Jessie and I decided it was about time we saw a few ships, so made our way to the harbour. Various ships were moored along the quay, others were standing off in the harbour. Some sailors were working on the quay and in the camaraderie of the same service, asked where we were stationed. When we explained how we were buried in the depths of the country and desperate for a sight of the sea and ships, they grinned and offered to show us their ship. Their ship turned out to be a cable layer which was moored alongside another by the jetty and if we cared to clamber over a few rails and across a couple of decks, they would be delighted to show us around.

They were as good as their word. They not only showed us over the ship, but introduced us to the chief engineer, an older man who explained to us the intricacies of his domain. The technicalities escaped me, but I did notice the huge roll of cable ready to be unrolled and laid upon the sea bed when the need arose. We were then treated to a large mug of cocoa each, the sailors staple beverage. We had a great time and left promising to meet our sailor friends at a dance later that day.

Unfortunately our forty-eight hour leave was soon over and Jessie and I had to return to Bletchley Park and duty once more, but our short break had given a real uplift to our spirits and was considered by us both as well spent.

Food for those in His Majesty's Forces was usually plentiful if somewhat uninteresting, the general type of menu consisting of foods that were filling rather than artistic in creation, but occasionally, for a special function the cooks surprised us by giving rein to their imagination and providing some delectable dishes. There were other times when the same ingredient occurred time and time again until we were heartily sick at the sight of it. Such was the case of the dried apricots.

It was a pleasant surprise when one day at the Bletchley Wrens' canteen we were given an apricot dessert. Fruit in wartime Britain was scarce and those more exotic fruits from the lands of sunshine were very rare indeed. To the civilian

population dried fruit was almost as precious as gold dust and had to be guarded and used most carefully. Even in the more privileged kitchens of the three services it was a rare treat, so when we were given apricots it was a happy day. Next morning we were still happy to be served apricots as an addition to our cereal, but when apricots appeared in various guises at every meal for over a week, happiness began to pall and we longed for a change. The final straw came when I went home on forty-eight hours' leave, looking forward to my mother's cooking, and she met me at the door saying, 'I have a special treat for your dinner. I managed to get some apricots!' Somehow I went right off apricots and remain so to this day!

The war continued, but with a more hopeful look for the Allies now. Gerry managed to get a long leave now and then. Sometimes I was able to arrange my leave for the same period and we were home together. Stationed in the remoteness of the Orkney Islands Gerry was completely out of touch with events taking place in the rest of Britain. When spending a day together in London, we were walking along the street when a doodlebug came over. People paused to listen and glance up at the sky before continuing on their way. Gerry looked puzzled.

'What's that noise?' he asked.

'A doodlebug,' I replied. 'Let's go down into the underground for a while.'

Gerry had never heard of the doodlebug and required an explanation.

'It's a flying bomb, Hitler's latest secret weapon. As long as you can hear its engine going you are okay but if the engine stops, dive for cover!'

These flying bombs or V1s, were aimed at no specific military targets, but were sent in an attempt to terrify the civilian population and were directed towards London. When they first began on 13 June 1944 they were a complete surprise. Looking like a small aircraft in the sky, people did not at first realise that there was no pilot aboard, only a deadly load of dynamite. When the population understood this new weapon they accepted them with resignation and carried on with their work. Later in the year, after the liberation of Paris and

Brussels by the Allied armies, Hitler let loose his second secret weapon, the V2. This was a rocket-bomb which gave no warning whatsoever, descending suddenly from the sky, blowing everything to 'Kingdom come' on impact. Stationed as we were in the heart of the country, it was only when I was home on leave that I saw the apprehension and destruction they caused. The last of these unholy weapons fell on 26 March 1945.

When going on long leave we were issued with ration cards for all the basic foods such as meat, butter, sugar, tea, etc. which was of some help to our families. An extra help were the dockets which were provided to Wrens to buy pyjamas or, better still, material with which to make pyjamas. These were very useful as all shops were very accommodating and did not insist on our buying the traditional striped material normally used for such garments, but were happy to sell any material we fancied, striped, flowered, polka-dotted or plain, cotton, woollen, linen, satin or lace as long as we could afford it. There were of course no man-made materials in the shops in those days. Nylon, the first of the man-made materials we were to see did not appear for sale until after the war. The dockets therefore enabled us to cast aside our uniform whilst on leave and appear in more feminine garb which brought a gleam to the boyfriend's eyes.

Hats, apart from uniform almost disappeared during the war years. Head scarves were adopted instead. Long hair was enclosed in snoods, a form of net often attractively coloured or decorated. These were originally introduced to avoid women factory workers catching their hair in machinery, but were then taken up as a patriotic fashion.

Make-up was short for most women, but we in the women's forces were luckier than most in that respect and were usually able to obtain what we required in our own stores. Fairly soon after I joined the WRNS we were allowed to use shoulder bags. Regulation navy blue, these were also sold in naval stores. They were a great help, as up until then, all our feminine bits and pieces had to be carried in pockets which did little to help the cut of our uniform or our personal shape. About this time also we were no longer compelled to wear the thick lisle issue stockings, but could wear black stockings made of artificial silk. Naturally we chose to wear the artificial silk. They may not have been long-lasting as they easily laddered, but they certainly made our legs more attractive and put us into fair competition with nurses who had always been allowed to wear them.

Another little perk we had in the women's services vital to our well-being, was that all sanitary towels were provided free due to the benevolence of Lord Nuffield; a basic need which saved us spending our meagre pay.

One complaint voiced by Wrens at Bletchley Park was that we had no category badge and were often mistaken for raw recruits by other members of the Royal Navy. Unless we had a badge of rank, such as an anchor, or hook as it was called, to show we were a leading Wren, we were frequently thought of as 'sprogs', that is a recruit of less than two or three weeks. We could see no reason why we should not have had some insignia to indicate some form of work, a 'Writers' badge would have done and would have prevented a lot of awkward questions being asked. As it was, when questions persisted, particularly from some of the USA forces who attended our dances, we resorted to spinning fantastic tales of a submarine which we kept in the lake of the grounds to try out various camouflage colourings. It was not until we came to talking of painting it purple with yellow spots, that they realised they were being 'led up the garden path' so to speak and we were not being serious. Our grievance on the lack of badges seemed perfectly reasonable as members of the army walked about with flashes on their shoulders marked 'INTELLIGENCE' and naval officers wore a pale green ring alongside their gold braid. We were left to rely on our imagination and feminine wiles to ward off any interest in our work from curious questioners. In spite of possible fifth columnists or quislings (the former describing persons working for the enemy and the latter describing traitors) the work at Bletchley Park remained the best kept secret of the war.

On the war fronts, from the beginning of 1942 things began to improve as far as the Allies were concerned. Hitler's army had been unable to break the Soviet people or contend with the harsh winter weather and on 31 January the remnants of the Sixth German Army surrendered at Stalingrad. In May the Royal Navy finally overcame the U-boat menace in the Atlantic and the army took the surrender of the Axis forces in Tunisia. The North African victory paved the way for an Allied landing in Sicily in July. In September they moved on to Italy and on 8 September Italy capitulated although the German forces fought on. In December the great German battleship the *Scharnhorst* was sunk and so another threat to shipping was removed.

The picture on the Far Eastern front was not so rosy and bright. The Japanese were tenacious and fanatical fighters. It had taken six months for combined Australian and American forces to win Guadalcanal. There was still much more fighting to take place before the Allies were to liberate all Japanese-occupied islands.

Back in Europe in January 1944 Allied troops landed at Anzio and after a hard struggle fought their way to Rome which they captured on 4 June. With the Normandy landings on 6 June we at last felt we were on the way to finishing the war and Victory. News was of course restricted by the censor but eagerly sought nonetheless. Those who had a chance to listen to radios passed on the details to others who had had no opportunity to tune in.

It took two long months of tough fighting before the Allied troops were to reach Paris, but on 25 August General de Gaulle of the Free French contingent at the head of a parade of Allied troops was able to enter Paris and walk its boulevards to the cheers of its liberated citizens. The jubilations were shown on the Pathé and Movietone newsreels in cinemas soon after the actual entry and lightened the hearts of us all. Our troops went on to free Brussels on 3 September to similar scenes of joy, but heartening as this was, the war was not yet won and we still had some hard work ahead of us.

Not long after the joyful euphoria on the liberation of Paris and Brussels, a setback occurred which made us realise that victory was not yet at hand. An attempt was made to shorten the course of the war by operation 'Market Garden'. This entailed the dropping of airborne troops near Arnhem in the Netherlands to seize the bridge over the River Rhine and the area surrounding it. At the same time a push would be made by armoured divisions of Allied troops to form a link from the Belgium front. The operation which took place from the 17–26 September 1944 failed, mainly due to the presence of some divisions of Hitler's battle hardened Panzer Corps recently moved to the Arnhem area from the Russian front. This was not taken into account by the British and American commanders at the time and as a result the operation was unsuccessful and many of our finest men were lost. Many brave Dutch people helped our men at the risk of their own lives.

A friend who was in the glider-borne regiment of the First Airborne Division gave this account:

> 'After a short briefing, the First Airborne Division were given the last bridge.'
> (There were three bridges involved in the planned attack.)
> 'We flew off on 17 September. It was a Sunday: glorious day of sunshine; the smoothest trip I had ever done; it wasn't bumpy.'

Those watching from the ground saw a tremendous armada of planes towing gliders gleaming in the sun against a clear blue sky. Each glider contained a platoon of thirty men and their equipment.

> 'We were in one of the first flights over and made a perfect landing. I was very glad to be in one of the first flights as the dropping ground wasn't very crowded. Later on a few did pile up on top of the others. We all got out without any trouble and were not fired upon. We managed to collect the platoon together. The parachutists were going for Arnhem bridge and our job was to hold the area and prevent the Germans getting in. So we set off on foot for a

123

village called Renkum where there was a ferry. We had a marvellous reception from the Dutch people, who turned out to greet us waving flags and giving us apples. At the ferry there were about nine German soldiers who immediately surrendered and we dug ourselves in on the banks of the Rhine.'

They were kept aware of the movements of the local German troops by the Dutch people in the nearby farmhouse. The farmers used the public telephone system to phone their police friends of the local town to gain information.

'We stayed there about thirty-six hours, until the Germans got their act together and we were mortared out of it. We had to withdraw. We lost our jeep transport and had to move back in the direction of Arnhem. For most of the time after that we were on what was called the perimeter, while the others were fighting for the bridge.'

Communications were very bad. Their wireless sets failed to work and groups were isolated, not knowing what other action was taking place in other sectors. They fell back to the village of Osterbeek, which was central to much of the fighting and dug in, in the garden of a family named Van Daalen. The information given at the briefing had been that there were only small parties of German troops; resting at Arnhem, and the Airborne Divisions would be relieved by other troops within forty-eight hours at the latest. The information was wrong.

'We were amazed to see Panzar tanks emerging from the trees and bearing down upon us. We had to retreat again into the perimeter and took up a position behind the gas-works and I lost touch with part of my platoon.'

There they stayed for nine days, gradually finding out who was on either side of them. A counter-attack was made by the

First Company of which they were unaware due to the poor communications. The RAF came across dropping supplies of hampers of food, unknowingly straight into the German zone. Our men had no real food for days.

'I can remember being in the ruins of a house and finding a jar of strawberries preserved in water. They weren't very nice to taste, but they were something to eat. It was infuriating watching the RAF coming over, not knowing, dropping the hampers and getting shot down for their trouble. I just wish they hadn't bothered to come!'

Some Dutch people helped out in a large house used as a hospital station, but most had very sensibly moved away from the areas of conflict. Later Polish troops also arrived in the area. Groups who had been cut off from their own command joined together with other groups in an *ad hoc* fashion.

'I ended up with a platoon of my own men, a few Poles and a few South Staffords. You just made up what you could. The battle went on around the perimeter without many people knowing what was happening. We certainly didn't know what was happening down at the bridge.'

It was not going at all well for the Allies down at the bridge and eventually after eight days of fighting, word came to withdraw the following morning. That meant crossing the River Rhine which was swift flowing and wide. Boats were required to take men across.

'The company commander came to see me and said, "Your orders are to stay and cover the withdrawal. One of the tapes (lines of men) will come through your area and your orders are to stay until they are withdrawn. Just before first light you can go." When everyone else had gone through, I sent my

125

own platoon down to the river. My batman had managed to find a boat. When everyone else had gone, I went to see if I could get across, but there was obviously no hope of that. I met up with a fellow subaltern and we decided to try and make a break for it and get through the German lines, but we were shot up and found ourselves rather ignominiously behind a pile of cow manure with a machine-gun the other side. We decided it was time to surrender.'

The perimeter which they were defending was a very small area which was heavily bombarded by German mortars. Although they managed to get the wounded out, the dead could not be moved. Casualties were high.

'We couldn't do any clearing up,' was the comment.

Morale remained good, however, the men defending their positions until ordered to withdraw.

'I felt so sorry for the Dutch. The enthusiasm they greeted us with on the 17th and the reprisals the Germans inflicted upon them only nine days later because of this enthusiasm.'

This account was given in a form of masterly under-statement of what must have been an intensely difficult and dangerous situation. Now, at Arnhem there is a museum, the Airborne Museum, which tells the story of this battle. The defeat of the operation sobered our elation causing us to renew our determination to work and fight even harder.

Troops invariably showed a sense of humour in the names they bestowed upon their vehicles, whether, tanks, trucks, planes or, in the above case, gliders, painting the names on the fuselage of the craft. One named 'Cherubs Chindits' was so called after the young and innocent-looking officer in charge of the platoon, nicknamed 'Cherub', by his messmates. Another named 'Bishop's Bashers' so named because its officer was known to be a churchman. A third was called 'The Things we do for George'.

A rather starchy, but puzzled staff officer inquired of the Corporal, 'Who is George?'

The Corporal, coming smartly to attention and saluting, said, 'His Majesty King George, sir,' leaving the staff officer lost for words.

9

One redeeming aspect about working at Bletchley and away from the main naval bases was that we rarely had to turn out for any form of muster or parade, so most of the drilling or 'square-bashing' we had done in training was unused in our present situation, for which we were grateful. If any parades did occur they must have taken place when I was on duty for I cannot remember taking part in any. The only time I had to muster was to collect my pay and that was a pleasure.

The American forces amazed and amused us with their form of marching parades. It seemed more like a dance with six steps forward, two back, about turn and face the way you had come, all done to music. All very entertaining, but a little devious if the purpose was to move a squad of men from one point to another in the shortest possible time. A kind of chorus chant appeared to be required to go with the movements. Maybe they did it just for fun? I think at the time we felt it was rather showy and out of place, but that was probably due to the 'no nonsense' attitude of our naval training.

During the late summer Gerry came home on leave. I managed to arrange some leave at the same time and we spent a few days with some friends of his near Dorking. These two middle-aged ladies ran a small residential school in a village set in beautiful countryside of woodland, hills and heath. Their little school had pupils of all ages from five to fifteen and must have been one of the last of the 'old dame schools'. The school was an old rambling thatched cottage with varying floor levels and winding stairs, but felt very cosy and homely. The children were happy, lively and seemed contented. I cannot comment, however, on their educational ability. The ladies were kindly, charming and made us very welcome. Gerry and I tried to repay their hospitality by keeping the children amused. In the evenings we joined the children in a game of cricket on the open heathland beside the school, which had us all laughing and happily tired by bed time. On Saturday afternoon the children had the choice of going to the cinema with their teachers or coming for a walk in the woods with us. Quite a number elected to come with us and had the time of their lives climbing trees and playing hide-and-seek. We enjoyed their company and everyone of those few days seemed full of sunshine.

Soon after that leave Gerry was reposted. After a spell of silence his letters again resumed as frequently as ever, but coming from Australia. No more shared leaves!

My work continued as usual. I had heard nothing further about my request for overseas service since entering the WRNS so I decided to jog someone's memory. I requested an interview with the WRNS officer in charge. This granted, I put forward my request for a posting overseas.

I was asked, 'Where have you in mind?' This surprised me, but ever-hopeful I replied 'Australia'.

Gerry's letters had of course sent me thinking in this direction, but I was also keeping up a correspondence with cousins in Melbourne and knew we had other family connections in several different parts of that country. I knew also that there were a number of naval bases there and I was still keen to get to a port, no matter how far. My request was noted; I was dismissed and that seemed to be the end of the matter.

Work remained the same routine, the only slight variation being that I was once suddenly asked to man the telephone switchboard at Stockgrove Park. The Wren on duty was taken ill unexpectedly and I happened to be the only Wren nearby at the time. My experience of such a job was nil, and all I had was a fifty second lesson before the said Wren was removed to sick-bay. I sat in the office praying nobody would ring, but of course they did. It had to be a call for our first officer! I looked at the array of wires and sockets before me, took a deep breath, crossed my fingers and plugged into the first socket I came to. Glory be! It was the right socket! Much to my relief, after half an hour or so another Wren of the regulating staff arrived to take over and I thankfully relinquished my post before confusion was caused in the quarters.

A welcome break in routine of work and rest occurred when Alan arrived unexpectedly at quarters one day. His ship had come home after eighteen months at sea in which he visited the West African coast among other ports and where he caught a dose of malaria. He had many interesting stories to tell of life at sea. I remember food or lack of food figured largely, including the unwelcome supplements of large numbers of weevils in the diet. It was a wonderful surprise to see him again, although for such a short time, as he had to return to his ship within a few days. He also caused quite a stir in the rarefied atmosphere of a WRNS quarters, amongst the other girls there. A real sailor was indeed unusual.

Twice I became an inmate of sick-bay whilst at Bletchley: once with an outbreak of impetigo for which I was isolated, and again for a bad attack of influenza. This could be quite a pleasant sojourn once the discomfort of the illness was over. Situated in a large and attractive country house with spacious gardens, the atmosphere was relaxed, the nurses friendly and not overworked. They found time to chat and discuss magazine articles with their patients, of whom there were usually few and those few not seriously ill. It was difficult for friends to visit those in sick-bay due to the problem of transport, but a couple of my friends managed it once during my recovery from influenza.

At home my parents were struggling to maintain a business in the face of numerous difficulties. Shortage of staff, shortage of stock to sell and irate customers were combined with days and nights disturbed by air-raids. Small rations, shortages of even the most basic vegetables, fruit and bread on which they had to rely for food, sapped energy and strength. As with all occupants of blocks of premises, Dad was obliged to take his turn in the rota of fire-watching. It was the fire-watcher's duty to be aware of, and immediately extinguish, any incendiary bombs dropped on buildings in his sector, before they had a chance to take hold and cause more serious fires. This required the watcher to be alert even though air-raids might not take place every night.

A further problem occurred in early summer when Cindy was taken ill at school. She turned out to have peritonitis and was rushed to hospital for an emergency operation. She was seriously ill for some time which was a tremendous worry for our parents. Happily Cindy recovered and Mother took her to Eire, Southern Ireland, to recuperate. Eire, being a neutral country, had no rationing and few restrictions. Cindy remembers this period as a very happy time spent with friends on a farm in beautiful and peaceful countryside, away from the terrors and grimness of wartime England.

Summer passed, Autumn arrived. There seemed to be a stalemate on the European front, our Allied troops advance slowed by the fierce resistance of the German forces. There was better news from the Pacific region where in October the Americans had relanded in the Phillipine Islands and where on 21–22 October there was a naval victory by USA forces against the Japanese at Leyte Gulf.

Rumours abounded in November 1944 that there had been an attempt on Hitler's life by some German generals. The attempt failed, the generals were punished and Hitler's rage was fanatical. Just before Christmas any complacency among the Allied nations was shattered by an unexpected offensive by Hitler's crack troops against the Allies in the Ardennes and Alsace. Many losses of men and armaments occurred on both sides and it seemed that our hopes of an ending to this long conflict were doomed, or at the very least considerably delayed. We set our minds to ploughing on through a tough winter of continuing hardships and disappointments, knowing that however difficult it was for us, it was far worse for those fighting in the front lines of battle.

Women continued to knit gloves and balaclava helmets to be sent to the servicemen to protect them from the Winter weather, although unable to offer them protection from the guns. On the home front Mother wrote to say that it was now almost impossible to obtain items such as toilet rolls and elastic, both being basic requirements for a lady's needs.

In January 1945 the Russians once again eased the pressure by launching a new attack along their eastern area of the European battleground, forcing Hitler to move many of his troops to that region. In spite of all Hitler's efforts the Russians made great advances and on 17 January took the Polish capital of Warsaw. The news cheered our Winter. Other bright days were when we heard of further advances in the Pacific, for in February, Americans took Manila, capital of the Phillipine Islands, and in March British troops recaptured Mandalay in Burma. Spring was a time of rejoicing when on 21 March British troops crossed the Rhine, and the end of this dreadful war seemed to be in sight. People listened eagerly to the broadcasts given by war correspondents such as Wynford Vaughan Thomas who gave such vivid descriptions of events from the front line of battle that we felt that we were sharing in their struggle. Our thoughts, prayers and every fibre of our bodies were willing them on in their task. Perhaps at last we were done with the 'Gremlins', those nasty little creatures who put a spanner in the works just when things seemed to be going well.

Many new slang words had appeared since 1939. Some were peculiar to a particular service. 'Gremlin' came from the RAF, as did 'prang' meaning a crash. 'Browned off' and 'chokka', both meaning 'fed up' or disgruntled, were used by the army and the navy, as was 'pukka', meaning very correct. Someone who was greedy was known as a 'gannet' in the navy, thus maligning the poor bird. 'Wizard', meaning anything from very good to wonderful, and 'duff gen', meaning poor information, both came from the RAF.

American slang also became widespread. 'Swell', a word notifying admiration or whole-hearted agreement, was often heard. Girls were referred to as 'chicks' or less complimentary, 'broads'. So 'a swell chick' was fine, 'a dumb broad' not so fine. Words we knew such as 'cute', which we understood as meaning 'sharp-witted' or clever, was used to convey attractiveness by our American friends. Thus a 'cute baby' was not a sharp-witted young child, but an attractive girl. New words made their appearance and stayed, becoming accepted as part of the new English language. Many others have been dropped, forgotten or replaced by fresh terms from new generations.

We were saddened by the news of the death of President Roosevelt on 12 April 1945. His health had been ailing for some time, as could be seen from photographs taken at the Yalta Conference and meeting with Churchill and Stalin. With his death Britain lost a good friend. Vice-President Harry Truman became President of the United States of America, maintaining the friendly relations established with his predecessor. Only a day or two after Roosevelt's death we heard that American forces had crossed the River Elbe and were close to closing the gap between the West Front and the Eastern Front advanced by the Russians.

There had been moves amongst the politicians of the Allied Countries to find some way to settle future disputes of the world before they flared into open conflict and caused further global wars. The League of Nations had not had much success, but there were always hopes that *this* time men would have realised the foolishness and wastefulness of war and be able to settle their disagreements sensibly in discussion. To this purpose the opening of the first conference of The United Nations took place at San Francisco on 25 April 1945. Human nature being as it is, many people like myself felt that national ambitions and pride would always prove a difficult if not impossible hurdle to overcome, but everyone felt we had to try for the sake of future generations.

Soon after we received the glad news that on 2 May the German forces in Italy had finally surrendered. Mussolini, who had been working with the Germans, was caught trying to flee. He was captured along with his mistress by Italian patriots who shot them and hung them both ignominiously by the side of the road.

On 3 May in Burma, Rangoon was retaken. Then on 5 May 1945 came the news that sent people singing and dancing in the streets: all German forces had surrendered unconditionally. The European war was over! 8 May was designated as V.E. Day. Victory in Europe. On that day immediately after Big Ben had struck the hour of 3 p.m., the BBC presenter John

Snagge announced that the prime minister, Winston Churchill, was to speak. A pause; then the voice we all knew so well delivered a most stirring speech.

'Yesterday morning at 2.41 a.m. at HQ General Jodl, the representative of the German High Command and Grand Admiral Doenitz, the designated. head of the German State, signed the act of unconditional surrender of all German land, sea and air forces in Europe to the Allied Expeditionary Force and simultaneously to the Soviet High Command. . . . Hostilities will end officially at one minute after midnight tonight but in the interests of saving lives the cease-fire began yesterday to be sounded all along the front and our dear Channel Islands are also to be freed today. The German war is therefore at an end.

After years of intense preparation, Germany hurled herself on Poland at the beginning of September 1939 and in pursuance of our guarantee to Poland and in agreement with the French Republic, Great Britain, the British Empire and Commonwealth of Nations, declared war upon the foul aggressor. . . . Finally almost the whole world was combined against the evil-doers who are now prostrate before us. . . .

We may allow ourselves a brief period of rejoicing; but let us not forget for a moment the toil and efforts that lie ahead. Japan with all her treachery and greed remains unsubdued. The injury she has inflicted on Great Britain, the United States, and other countries, and her detestable cruelties, call for justice and retribution. We must now devote all our strength and resources to the completion of our task, both at home and abroad. Advance Britannia! Long live the cause of freedom! God Save the King.'

His unmistakable voice and eloquent phrases were broad-

134

cast throughout the country and relayed through loudspeakers in most cities of Britain. When Mr Churchill had finished speaking the last post was sounded, a tribute to all those who had given their lives in the cause of liberty and freedom. It was a very moving moment. The national anthem was played to end this momentous and historic broadcast.

People celebrated the end of conflict in their own individual way. Of course there was much rejoicing. Crowds flocked to Buckingham Palace where during the afternoon at about 4.30 p.m. the Royal Family, accompanied by Winston Churchill, stepped on to the balcony to the cheers of the people massed outside the gates and railings. A few more agile members of the public even perched upon the statue of Queen Victoria to obtain a better view. King George VI was in naval uniform but bare-headed, Princess Elizabeth was in the uniform of the ATS and the Queen and Princess Margaret were dressed in blue, thus representing the colours of all three armed services.

Flags and bunting were brought out of store to decorate the street and war-scarred buildings. Famous landmarks of London's Big Ben, Buckingham Palace, the National Gallery, St Paul's Cathedral, were all floodlit and searchlights were switched on to form an arc of light over London city. People lit huge bonfires in celebration to add to the brightness of the night and kissed and danced with complete strangers. For those who wished to give their thanks in a quieter way and to remember those whom they had lost, informal services were held throughout the day in St Paul's.

All this I heard and saw later on radio and newsreels. Celebrations took place everywhere in Britain, but strangely enough I cannot remember taking part in any although I am sure there must have been some form of party or dance at our quarters to note the occasion. However, I do remember feeling that a great burden, or load that had been hanging over us all like a dark shadow, had been lifted and a sense of freedom pervaded our spirits. After six years of frustration and fear, the release was almost unbelievable. We needed time to adjust to the new circumstances.

In Germany there was a rash of suicides among the leading

members of the Nazi party. The self-styled Führer, Adolf Hitler, the cause and instigator of the world war and Eva Braun, his mistress recently made his wife, committed suicide in the well-fitted underground bunker in Berlin before the conquering Allied troops could reach them. Goebbels, his propaganda minister, a stranger to truth, and Himmler, Hitler's deputy, followed his example. Hermann Goering was captured and sentenced to death in the Nuremberg trials which came after the round-up of Nazi criminals, but committed suicide in prison in 1946 before the sentence could be carried out. At the Nuremberg trials in 1946 Rudolf Hess was committed to life imprisonment and died in Spandau Fortress Prison in 1987, the only remaining prisoner there. Spandau jail was then in the Russian sector of Germany.

Although the actual fighting in Europe was over, there was much clearing up to be done. As Allied troops made their way through Germany, releasing prisoners of war, political prisoners and others, the Russian forces pushed on to Berlin, taking the German capital and all land to the east of it under their control.

It was not until the surrender of Germany to the Allies, which was ratified in Berlin on 9 May 1945, and the tidying up process across the country began, that the full horror of Hitler's regime was known. It was then that the terrible concentration camps crowded with the hapless victims of the Nazi persecution and extermination policy were discovered. The liberating soldiers were appalled at the dreadful conditions they found: people who were no more than walking skeletons, men, women and children, not only physically starved, but deprived of all human dignity and consideration. The non-survivors were buried in mass graves where they had been thrown piled one on top of another in their hundreds. Names such as Belsen and Auschwitz sent shudders of horror down the spines of all decent people. It was almost unbelievable that members of a so-called civilised nation could have perpetrated such degradation and sadistic cruelty on other human beings, but the proof was there for all to see. As further horrors were uncovered they were documented and filmed and in due course some were shown on cinema screens in Britain and countries all over the world, shocking everyone into an awareness of the extreme evil of the Nazi ideology.

Just before the final collapse of Germany, the British government had decreed it sufficiently safe to lift certain restrictions and on 20 April 1945 the blackout was ended. At the time I was spending a forty-eight hour leave in Cambridge staying at the YWCA hostel. It was my first visit to the city and I set out to explore its streets and historic buildings. In doing so I happened to meet an American GI with the same purpose. In the easy camaraderie of those wartime days we chatted and continued to explore the town together. We were strolling along one of the main streets in the early evening when suddenly all the lights came on and Cambridge was sparkling with street lamps aglow. Lamps unused for so long were now casting their beam onto the streets and pavements once again. As we watched, further lights appeared at doors and windows. The town seemed to grow and glow out of the darkness.

My companion stopped and said, 'Gee, I haven't seen lights like this for two years.'

I reminded him that it was six years since I had last seen them!

The end of blackout not only lightened our streets, but lightened our hearts too. It was a positive indication that the fear of night-raids was over and life would improve. We could look forward to happier times.

Although hostilities were at an end in Europe, the fight against the Japanese in the Far East still continued and all our energies were now concentrated in this theatre of war. Once the tidying up of German signals was completed, the code-books all in Allied hands, there was little work for the Wrens and staff in that section to do, therefore we received orders to transfer to the Japanese sector. Where the Germans had been methodical and organised in their approach, the Japanese seemed haphazard and confusing. No sooner did our navies sink such and such a *maru* and cross it off the list of shipping, then the name again appeared on signals in a completely different area. The Japanese simply attached the same name to another ship.

This meant that in our indexing we needed to double-check everything to be sure we fitted the signals to the correct vessel. Gradually I adapted to this new area of work where the frequency of signals did not appear to be as great as those we had been used to in the European theatre, although they were more complicated. Possibly the comparative lack in numbers was due to the great distance involved and to the greater involvement of our American allies in this sector of war.

It was not the policy of the Japanese fighting man to surrender, for to them this was an act to dishonour their name and so they tenaciously and viciously fought every step of the way from island to island as they retreated in the advance of the Allies. On 10 June Australian forces landed in Borneo and with the help of the local Dyak population proceeded to drive the enemy from the jungle-covered island.

The Pacific area of war was a different and more difficult form of fighting from that of the European continent. On land most of the fighting consisted of seeking the enemy in areas of jungle or bush where the trees and plants grew so thickly that men were unable to see their own comrades let alone a well-hidden enemy. Added to this was the steamingly hot and humid climate with all the disadvantages of unpleasant and irritating insects, plus ill health from malaria and other debilitating tropical diseases and sores. Supplies were also more difficult to transport and therefore news and film coverage of happenings did not reach the general public very frequently. Men from the Far Eastern section complained afterwards that they were the 'Forgotten Army'.

My work at Bletchley with the Far East Japanese section continued for another month or two when I was then given a long leave. Telephoning to mother first to warn her of my imminent homecoming, I packed my small attaché case, collected my railway warrant and set off for Bletchley station. To reach the station Wrens either had to take the bus transporting those to duty at Bletchley Park or hitch-hike our way there. Most girls arranged to start their leave after completing a weeks' watch and went directly from work.

My parents and Cindy gave me a warm welcome home and I

looked forward to ten days' relaxation and the chance to get out of uniform for a while. Britain was enjoying a spell of summer sunshine and it was pleasant to walk about the village chatting with old friends and acquaintances. Not many of my young contemporaries were home, but chatting to their parents helped to bring me up-to-date with their movements.

A couple of days after I was home I received a telephone call from a Canadian I had met some weeks before. He had obtained my phone number from a friend and asked if we could meet. Knowing my father to have a close affection for Canada, I thought he might like to meet and talk to Ted, so I asked if he could join us at home for a day. My parents agreed and Ted was pleased to accept the invitation. Accordingly he came down next day and was introduced to the family. Ted, a member of the Canadian Air Force, was on leave in London. It was often a lonely time for members of overseas forces unless they had made friends with British families, as it meant lodging in the various hostels run for the services. These were comfortable and well-provided on the whole, but could not supply or make up for the family life many of them missed so much. We made no special arrangements except for mother who managed to make the rations stretch for one extra person. I had already given her my ration card which helped a little towards the catering.

Since 5 May life in the civilian world had become a little more relaxed. The tension and fear had eased, everyone was able to look forward to quiet nights, enabling the body to rest after a day's labour. Goods and food were still in short supply and there were still many restrictions, but apart from the lifting of the blackout regulations, some of the beaches had been cleared of barbed wire entanglements and explosive mines and were once again open to the general population to enjoy the benefits of sea and shore. Seaside shops went through their storerooms and found buckets and spades, hidden in dark recesses for the duration of war. These were brought out, put on display for sale and a new generation of children discovered the delights of sandcastles and rock pools.

The day with Ted was spent showing him something of

English home and village life. The evening was passed in a good old-fashioned way by us all gathering around the piano to play and sing songs until it was time for Ted to catch his train back to London. He must have enjoyed his time with us for he asked if he could come again.

Halfway through my leave I received another telephone call. This time it was an official one. My WRNS officer was recalling me back to duty the next day. I could not understand why and no reason was given. Early the following morning a telegram arrived confirming the telephone call. I had no option but to obey. My parents were disappointed that I had to return to Bletchley so soon. I was also disappointed and mystified as this had never happened to me before. However, I packed my bag and went as ordered. On my arrival at Stockgrove Park I was requested to report to the officer in charge and from her discovered the reason for my recall. My request had been granted. I was to be sent overseas! There was no information as to where I was to be sent as yet, but it was a reasonable guess that it would not be the European sector since hostilities were now at an end in that area. The officer then passed me another railway warrant, told me I had a week's embarkation leave and wished me luck.

As I would not be returning to Stockgrove Park, it meant collecting together all my kit and personal belongings and arranging for my bike to be sent home. It also meant saying goodbye to friends made over the last year or two. Some who were on watch I could not see, but left messages to be passed on. My first action had been to telephone Ted to let him know where I was. Having done everything necessary, I arranged a lift on the duty bus to pick up the next available train out of Bletchley station. It was a surprise to find Ted at Bletchley station waiting for me. To arrive so promptly he must have left London as soon as he received my message. I was glad of his company to share the exciting anticipation of my new orders – and to help carry my kit!

My parents were not so thrilled at my news, but accepted it as inevitable. They did their best to make my leave a happy one. I needed to buy a few off-duty clothes suitable to wear in a hot climate: that was the only clue we had to my destination. Mother offered to pay for them as the fourteen shillings a week Wren's pay would not stretch far in that direction, even with the addition of the higher specialist pay I was getting at that time. Between us we managed to find enough clothing coupons. I was able to help out with my pyjama dockets. To this end we spent a day together in London going around the shops.

Goods for sale may not have been as numerous as pre-war, but there was still a fair choice, even of such items as evening dresses. Now that the fear of bombing was over people were able to enjoy evening entertainments once more. Women welcomed a chance to dress up; to feel glamorous again and, judging by the reactions, their efforts were appreciated by the male population.

Ted spent one or two days with us before he had to return to his unit. During that time we experienced the joy-rides and side-shows of a country fairground, taken out of mothballs, its paint work touched up; its steam-engines hissing; its highly decorated roundabouts of bobbing wooden horses with brass poles gleaming in the sun; its swing boats; the big dipper with its switchback railway; all filling the air with the loud and lively music of steam-organs, competing with the raucous shouts of the showmen and women at the coconut-shy and other side-shows.

Ted was also introduced to the quieter delights of the village fête complete with competitions, stalls and maypole dancing by the local school children, where he met our local Baptist church minister. Such were the highlights of village life we enjoyed during those summer days after VE Day (Victory in Europe Day) 8 May 1945.

Time was spent by me saying goodbye to friends still at home; preparing myself for the coming adventure; collecting together small items I might need and getting my kit cleaned and neatly packed into the ungainly and awkward kit-bag, in which all non-commissioned members of His Majesty's forces were obliged to carry their gear. If incorrectly folded and packed, one's second uniform would emerge a crumpled mess,

141

catching the eye of one's superior officer, bringing the said officer's wrath upon one's head! Commissioned officers in the naval service were provided with suitcases of a rather attractive green textured material in which to transport their kit and belongings. I never attained such luxury.

Towards the end of my leave I received a brief telegram telling me to report to New College by such and such a time and day. At least I was on familiar ground here arriving complete with kit-bag attaché-case, shoulder-bag and gas-mask on a warm summer's day having somehow managed to transport it all on buses and the London underground system to the doors of New College regulating office. The one trunk I was allowed to take was sent on by rail. On settling in to this temporary abode, I met up with a number of other Wrens also on a list for embarkation overseas. Among them was Eileen, a girl I recognised as coming from Bletchley Park. We appeared to be the only two Wrens going from our section and although we had not known one another well, we were at least familiar faces and shared the anticipation and joy of the prospect of adventure before us, almost bubbling over in our excitement.

10

Altogether there were about forty to fifty Wrens awaiting embarkation at New College, all eager to know what our destination was to be. In the meantime we were subjected to medical examinations and inoculations, among other checks. One by one, arms bared and hands on hips, we passed by the barrier of nurses and doctor awaiting us, swabs and hypodermic needles at the ready, to receive inoculations for typhoid, typhus, tetanus, cholera and smallpox. The effects of this multiple inoculation were very obvious the following morning at roll-call when it was obligatory to fall in to attention on parade before the duty officer. While the roll was being called several of the girls fell out, flat on their faces! They were going down like nine-pins one after the other and were carted off to the sickbay. Those of us who survived the parade were detailed off to empty and refill with fresh water all the fire buckets standing ready for emergencies throughout the college. With our arms feeling sore, hot and swollen, we thought this a sadistic exercise and wished we had joined our fainting companions, but no doubt it was done with the intention of dispersing the effects of the jabs as quickly as possible.

A few days later we were once more called together and this time we had the news we had been awaiting and speculating on since the orders for embarkation leave had been received; our destination: Ceylon! That exotic and fabulous island of the Far East, the Tear Drop at the Foot of India; the Pearl of the Orient; the original garden of Eden. All these names had been applied to this mountainous island in the Indian Ocean.

Having given a few seconds for this momentous news to sink in, the officer continued with details of preparation for

143

embarkation. All Wrens had to be fitted with tropical kit, white skirts and short-sleeved white blouses, white canvas shoes, white socks, white belt and white hat. White underwear in 'blackout' style was also available. Needless to say, it received the same treatment as its navy counterpart! We were also issued with a pair of navy bell-bottom trousers with interesting flaps and fastening arrangements and a large sweater or jersey. Lectures on living in a tropical environment were also given with hints on health. All were kept fully occupied for the following few days. The destination had to be kept secret so we were confined to quarters and letters censored as normal.

Although the German U-boat scare was no longer a threat, the Japanese were still very active and troop-ships would be an obvious target, hence the need for secrecy. I was not aware at this time, but discovered after the war, that one of my friends from the village, also in the WRNS who had been sent overseas at an earlier date, had been aboard a troop-ship that had been torpedoed off the coast of Africa. She was lucky enough to survive as she had her lifebelt with her at the time when the torpedo struck and was picked up by another vessel, but many of her companions were lost.

Eventually embarkation day arrived. Naval trucks carried us with all our kit through London to Waterloo Station. The station platforms appeared to be a seething mass of men and women in the various uniforms of all the Allied services, most of whom were carting their heavy and awkward items of kit around with them, resembling overloaded mules. On the platform to which we were assigned stood squads of marines and naval personnel, a few nurses and one or two other 'odd bods'. We wove our ungainly way between them, kit-bags on shoulders, shoulder-bags and gas-masks dangling impeding our progress, to a section where we were instructed to await the arrival of the train.

It was not long in coming. Settling into our carriage carefully segregated from the marines and sailors, we stowed our luggage then watched the organised activity of others boarding this second stage to adventure. The small group of nurses and 'odd bods' had already disappeared from the platform, but the

144

large numbers of men and equipment involved required a little longer time. At last the platform was clear and the train slowly jolted its way out of the station on track to Southampton. Keeping our excitement under quiet control, mainly due to the presence of the petty officers among us, we chatted or gazed out at the scenery over the two hour journey. As the train drew into Southampton we saw the docks come into view and caught glimpses of funnels and masts of ships of many shapes and sizes appearing above and between the dock buildings. One of these was destined to carry us on stage three of our travels to the tropical island of Ceylon, now known as Sri Lanka. 'Lanka' was the original name of the Sinhalese kingdom and the Royal Navy used the same name for its base there, so on our documents our posting was to HMS *Lanka.*

We craned our necks to try to pick out this transport of delight. It was not until the train halted and we were formed into groups to be conducted down walkways to a covered area overlooking one of the docks, that we saw the SS *Esperance Bay.* She was a rather small and unimposing merchant vessel as she lay moored alongside. No luxury liner for us, but this cargo liner steam ship of 14,204 tons was to take us to our heart's desire, so we examined her bulk with avid interest. Baggage and stores were already being loaded. Dock workers and crew were busily making ready for her departure. Soon, the marines and sailors started to make their way up the gangway to the open doors in the ship's side. The nurses used a higher gangplank leading on to the deck. Our watching was interrupted by our petty officer calling us to attention. Picking up our kit-bags we followed the nurses setting foot on board the ship that was to be our quarters for the next few weeks.

Detailed off, five to each cabin originally intended for two, did not allow much room for movement, but we were to discover that we were infinitely better off than the marines and sailors consigned to the hold for their sleeping quarters. We at least had a porthole which gave us light and a view of the outside if only of sea and sky, although our deck being only just level with the water line and having a double tier of bunks against it, it was impossible to open. My cabin companions,

Eileen, Audrey and I came to an agreement on which bunk we should occupy. I started off on the top bunk, changing after the first week to the centre one and the following week to the bottom bunk, so that each of us had a fair share of sleeping on top and bottom bunks. Jane and Ethel worked in a similar system on the other side of the cabin. The cabin provided a wash-basin and mirror. Under the wash-basin was a small cupboard in which resided two small metal basins with handles on either side. These seemed rather ominous so we hastily shut them away, praying that we would never need to use them.

Once our gear was stowed we started to explore. Just along the companionway from our cabin we found the toilets and showers. On the deck above was the Wrens' mess-room. In peacetime this was the first-class dining-saloon. The officers and nurses also used the same mess, having the first sitting while the Wrens were called for the second sitting. The men had other mess rooms in different parts of the vessel. Our relaxation time was to be confined to the main deck which we shared with the men, officers and nurses sharing the smaller upper deck.

Within an hour or two of boarding, the ship was ready to sail. All gathered on deck lining the rails to say a last goodbye to England as the *Esperance Bay* left port and we watched the outline of the buildings and finally the shores fade into the distance. As we felt the vibrations of the engines and the swell of the waves of the open sea, we knew that we had embarked at last on the longest and most dangerous part of our journey. The fact that it was also the most uncomfortable we had yet to discover.

In a day or so the negotiation of companionways, stairs and decks were mastered without difficulty, our issue of bell-bottomed trousers proving useful in maintaining our modesty. Some talks on safety on board ship and other matters were arranged and for a few days we attended keep-fit sessions on deck given by a marine sergeant from which we staggered back to our bunks with aching limbs or collapsed on deck where we were, unable to reach the comfort of the bunk. Looking back, they probably were not all that tough, but although young, we were out of practice with much physical activity, having been confined to a sedentary job for the last year or two. As it was, some of the girls complained and the sessions were stopped which was a pity as there was little else to occupy our time.

The occasional amusing incident occurred to cheer us. The various groups took their meals separately. We sat at long tables in the mess. At the head of each table sat a petty officer. Swing-doors led to the galley or kitchens through which the ship's stewards came with the food on trays finely balanced on each hand to counteract the movement of the ship. We had completed our main course and the stewards had just begun to serve the dessert which on this day was blancmange and jelly. Several trayloads had been delivered safely when an agile and busy young steward came sailing through the swing-doors, trays held high, put his foot on a spot of blancmange carelessly dropped by a colleague. The ship rolled. The steward, one leg high in true ballet style, slid clear across the deck with great panache to land, not so gracefully, to the accompaniment of clattering trays and dishes, in an ungainly heap colourfully decorated with pink blancmange and red jelly. Not a single girl laughed or even tittered. We had only been on board a few days at this time and were still very wary of our new officers and strict discipline. As it was, a complete silence was maintained until the poor man had recovered himself and retreated to the galley. It would probably have been far less embarrassing for him had we all had a thoroughly good belly-laugh.

Through chatting to a member of the crew I discovered that the ship the *Esperance Bay* on which we travelled was sister ship to HMS *Jervis Bay* a ship which had achieved fame earlier in the war through the brave action of her crew. The *Jervis Bay* was a mixed passenger-cargo liner of 14,164 tons which was requisitioned for naval service on 25 August 1939 and commissioned as an armed merchant cruiser on 23 September at London. During October the *Jervis Bay* was on convoy duty in the Atlantic escorting a convoy of thirty-eight merchant ships from Halifax, Canada to the UK when on the afternoon of 5 November 1940 with the convoy proceeding at nine knots, a ship was sighted to the northward and then recognised as a warship, unfortunately an enemy warship, approaching rapidly.

Jervis Bay went to action stations, reporting the enemy and hoisted the signal 'prepare to scatter'. The oncoming ship was identified as a pocket battleship, the *Admiral Scheer* on a raiding foray in the Atlantic. The *Admiral Scheer* opened fire at about 17,000 yards distance and the convoy was immediately ordered to scatter and make smoke to cover their movements and confuse enemy fire. Meanwhile the *Jervis Bay* under the command of Acting Captain ESF Fegen RN had turned the *Jervis Bay* directly towards the enemy at her maximum speed of 5 knots, dropping smoke floats as she went.

The German ship was much more heavily armed with six 11 inch and eight 5.9 inch guns directed by very modern fire-control equipment. The *Jervis Bay* had only seven old 6 inch guns in open single mountings whose maximum range was 14,000 yards. It was unlikely she could ever get within shooting range of her adversary. Moreover, she was completely un-armoured and with her low speed she was virtually a sitting duck. She could be likened to a cocker spaniel in a fight with an alsatian.

The first hits put her fire-control gear out of action and wrecked the bridge, and she was soon reduced to a blazing shambles. The engagement commenced at 17.10 local time and the *Jervis Bay* was last seen two hours later still burning and went down with her colours flying. She had done her job. In forcing the *Admiral Scheer* to concentrate attention upon her, she gave the merchant ships more time to scatter and also reduced the period of daylight available to the enemy to pursue the other ships.

The *Admiral Scheer* sank five other ships at that time and a neutral Swedish ship three days later, but thirty-one of the original convoy reached port safely. Without the brave action of the *Jervis Bay* and her crew it may have been a lot less. Of the crew thirty-four officers including the captain and one hundred and fifty-six men lost their lives. Sixty-five survivors were picked up by the Swedish ship *Stureholm* which returned to the scene on sighting a distress signal flashed from a raft. Captain

Fegen of the *Jervis Bay* was posthumously awarded the Victoria Cross.

For the first week or so our journey on the *Esperence Bay* was punctuated by sightings of other vessels and on crossing the Bay of Biscay, mercifully calm at the time, although even some of our marines succumbed to attacks of *mal de mer*. We saw the rocky points of Gibraltar and the British naval base there. Glimpses of the North African coast appeared, hazy and hot in the warmth of a Mediterranean summer. It was at this stage that the order for rig of the day changed to whites or tropical gear. We Wrens were glad to discard our thicker uniforms and try out the white skirts, cut in panels which gave us more freedom than the tight navy skirts. White short-sleeved blouses with V-necks were much more comfortable than the white shirts, separate collars and ties of the normal uniform. Black stockings were also put aside. Instead we wore white socks and white canvas shoes. The men's gear consisted of short-sleeved shirts with shorts, in khaki for the marines and white for the sailors. This gave everybody the chance to 'get their knees brown' as the expression went, and avoid arriving among tanned, seasoned troops looking pale, wan and obvious newcomers.

British service shorts were notorious for their length and bagginess. Some of the men hit upon the idea of asking the girls on board to shorten them. One rather well-built young man requested my help in this matter and showed where he wanted them cut. I felt this was a little excessive, but he was adamant that they should be cut at this point, so cut them I did and neatly hemmed the edges before returning them. A few days later I noticed a group of men on deck who appeared to be ribbing one of their members. Their target was my rotund and embarrassed friend now wearing his very short shorts revealing rather more than he had anticipated and barely maintaining the necessary modicum of decency. In 1945 forms of dress were not as liberated as they are in the 1990s and I dare not think what his sergeant said!

Sailing through the Mediterranean Sea was a pleasant experience now that threat of attack from Germany and Italy

149

was over. At Port Said the bum-boats came out to meet us, their shallow crafts filled with items for sale: leather goods of all kinds, carvings, jewellery and even rugs and carpets. They crowded alongside the hull of our ship, flinging ropes up over the rail to form a pulley on which to raise their baskets of wares, shouting in competition with one another to attract our custom. The colour, frantic activity and noisiness of the scene made a welcome change from the inactivity of the previous days, but unfortunately for the occupants of the bum-boats we were not good customers as we had received no pay since leaving England and had no money with which to buy their goods.

All personnel were confined to the ship and as soon as the ship had received fresh supplies, the captain was eager to be on his way once more. The *Esperance Bay* joined a convoy of other vessels awaiting passage through the Suez Canal and before long we were enclosed within its narrow confines and on either side instead of limitless sea we viewed the sun baked earth of desert lands and sands. On the Egyptian side this was softened by the green of areas of cultivation and habitation where robed figures moved or sat in the shade of the occasional group of palm-trees. Here also we saw camels in their natural environment and not as exhibits in a zoo. A few flat-roofed houses stood back from the canal bank. At various points along the bank of the canal on the Egyptian side, British soldiers waved, whistled and called out greetings yelling, 'You're going the wrong way!' Now that the European war was over they were keen to return home.

Once through Suez, and into the Red Sea our cramped accommodation began to tell. The stifling heat reflected from a glassy sea with not the wisp of a breeze to ruffle its surface had us gasping for air. It was uncomfortable for we girls in our small cabins, but that was nothing compared to the discomfort of the men packed in tiers in the hellish heat of the hold. It became an effort to lift a hand or blink an eyelid. Other little problems occurred to plague us such as infections of athlete's foot, a nasty little fungus which caused the skin to peel from between one's toes and a soreness to develop, or prickly-heat which caused a rash of madly irritating red spots under the armpits, breasts or other places where sweating occurred. Showers did little to relieve the problems, as the sea-water and latherless soap left one feeling only slightly cooler, but still sticky from the salt.

During this period I went to seek some advice from sick-bay and found the nurses there harassed and concerned over the condition of a stoker fireman member of the crew. He was suffering badly from heat exhaustion and they feared for his life. There were still several days sailing ahead of us before we could expect to leave the Red Sea area and the sun continued to blaze down upon us without relief from even the hint of a breeze. Sadly, despite all efforts of the medical staff the fireman died next day. A funeral service was held on deck and his body committed to the sea in the time-honoured way. A collection was made by some of the troops on board for the family of the dead man and we gave what money we could. Death has a sobering effect and the ship was very quiet for the next day or two despite the presence of over 1,500 people aboard her.

The comparative coolness of the night once the sun had set encouraged the men to leave the hold and sleep on deck instead. It was worth running the risk of a wet hose-down in the early morning when the decks were cleaned, to escape the stifling atmosphere of the hold.

To the whole-hearted thankfulness of everyone on board we finally left the Red Sea and its merciless heat behind us and sailed into the wider boundaries of the Indian Ocean. The breeze was welcomed as a long-lost friend. Frayed tempers returned to normal and reasonable contentment prevailed. Flying fish appeared, skimming over the waves like miniature rainbows. Groups of dolphins raced and leaped alongside and ahead seeming to encourage us on our way. At night the movement of the ship caused bright lights of fluorescence to appear on the surface of the water in a magical luminosity. Under the brilliance of the stars in cloudless skies we resumed our evening gatherings and sing-songs on deck. I was some-times asked to sing solos and usually sang folk-songs or popular ballads, a number of Irish ones among them, the 'Rose of

Tralee' being a favourite. After the first evening when I had sung, I was regaled when walking on deck by groups of marines who indicated that they recognised me by softly humming the tune of 'The Rose of Tralee' when I was near.

These sing-songs were one of the few entertainments possible on such a crowded ship and helped to relax tensions of the day. One other means of entertainment allowed by the navy was tombola. This number game took a similar form to 'Lotto', housey-housey or bingo which is the popular name nowadays. It involved covering the numbers on a card as the caller picks them from a bag or box. Concentration was called for and quietness descended on deck while the game was played. No gambling was allowed on board, but card-games were permitted and groups of men whiled away a few hours in a friendly game.

Space was at a premium. The only place to sit was on the wooden deck or on the hatchways to the hold, raised a little above deck level and therefore slightly more comfortable. The sunny skies, tempered by warm gentle breezes and accompanied by calm seas, made for perfect cruising weather. By closing your eyes and using a little imagination, you could shut out the hard and crowded deck, the threat of mines, torpedoes and enemy submarines and believe yourself on a luxurious liner sailing peacetime oceans. The warmth of the sun, the tang of the sea, the gentle swell of the waves and the background sound and vibration of the ship's engine were all there, only the material comforts were lacking. In this relaxed and indolent climate casual friendships were formed among shipmates, though few extended to surnames. The tropical clear and starry nights encouraged a few romantic attachments, but the ten o'clock curfew kept all within bounds and a cuddle and a kiss in the shadow of a lifeboat was as far as things went.

One unpleasant incident occurred which raised my hackles. A number of marines and Wrens were sitting on the foredeck enjoying the sunshine and chatting together, myself among them, when I noticed the quartermaster on the bridge trying to attract the attention of someone on the crowded deck. His signals seemed to be directed towards our group and not just

ALL ABOARD

153

our group, but towards me. I could not think why. However, I left the group and went to meet him. Imagine my horror when he abruptly accused me of setting fire to a lifeboat! He said he had seen me flick a cigarette end over the ship's side to land in one of the lifeboats. I denied knowledge of any such thing and as far as I could remember I had not been smoking. He accused me of lying and without further warning I was marched off to see the first officer. My friends were unaware of what was happening and I was given no chance to speak to them. I was beginning to feel extremely angry, but knew that I must keep such feelings under control or I would be in even more trouble. According to naval regulations I was marched up before the first officer who sat behind his desk in one of the ship's offices, where I was compelled to stand to attention while the quartermaster made his accusation. I was unable to speak without permission from the officer and only to answer questions put to me. When I was asked if the charge was true I could only answer, 'No, Sir'. They were the only words I was given a chance to say, I may have convinced the first officer, I don't know. He looked at me steadily and just as steadily I looked back, trying to keep my sense of outrage under control. Finally he spoke to the quartermaster, 'Muster all the Wrens on deck. I will speak to them'. Then to me, 'Dismiss'.

Puzzled Wrens were then assembled on deck in ranks, commanded to stand at ease and then subjected to a lecture on the danger of fire on board ship, while all the rest of the personnel on board watched and listened. It was a humiliating experience for us, especially as we were not to blame. One of the marines was decent enough to go to the first officer (or 'Jimmy the One' as naval slang termed the first officer) and confess it must have been he who flicked the cigarette and that he was unaware of where it had landed. I remained furious with the quartermaster who had accused and refused to believe me, but if I had hopes for an apology I was disappointed for no apology was forthcoming. I assumed he did not like Wrens, particularly those aboard his ship.

This unpleasant episode over, we settled back to a routine as normal as possible in the circumstances. There were no ports of call or sights of land from leaving the Red Sea all the way across the Indian Ocean until we should reach Colombo in Ceylon, only vast expanses of salt-water with the flying fish and dolphins to keep us company by day and the stars and moon by night.

To break the monotony a ship's concert was organised. I was asked to take part and sing for them. It occurred to me that it might be a nice change for the men to see someone out of uniform and I applied for permission to obtain my evening-dress from my trunk. This entailed entering the hold where our trunks were stowed, identifying my trunk from among a hundred others and removing it in order to open it and abstract the dress. The crew member detailed to help me do this was not too happy about it, and when we entered the hold I could understand why. Having made our way down numerous metal ladders to the bowels of the ship, the wave of heat which hit us as we walked into the hold was suffocating and we were both soon clammy and dripping in sweat. However, the trunks were so neatly stowed that I was able to recognise mine almost at once and the crewmen quickly had it out and open. Just as quickly I removed the dress and the trunk was replaced. We then left the hold and returned as fast as possible to the cooler areas of the ship.

Due to the crowded situation on board, rehearsals were difficult to arrange, so the concert was produced with a minimum of preparation. The actual performance took place on the open deck in the bow of the ship by the light of the moon and stars. Men with any form of musical instrument were persuaded to display their talents. Others got together in comedy acts or sang and two other Wrens sang a duet in harmony. When my turn came I stood in the well of the deck, the superstructure of the ship rising high above me and all around were the indistinct forms of men, sitting, squatting, perched or standing in any convenient space to be found. Above where the shadowy faces of men and Wrens leaning over the railing of the main deck and above them the even more indistinct shadows of the nurses and officers of the upper deck. I was grateful for the darkness that prevented my seeing any

155

face clearly, but I forgot them all as I lost any shyness in the music of the song. My only thought before I started was the hope that my unaccompanied voice was strong enough to carry the distance and would not be wafted away by the night's slight breeze.

A few days after the concert we woke one morning to find our ship anchored in the harbour of Colombo. Around us were moored other ships of all types and sizes. The sea was a slately colour, reflecting the sky above covered by a mantle of grey clouds. These clouds were releasing a shower of rain which hit the sea around us like spatters of small sharp pellets, each forming its own personal pool on the surface of the sea. Naturally, the deck was also under attack from these heavenly missiles and it was necessary to retrieve our raincoats from our kit-bags before venturing in to the open. The rain was a surprise, the first we had met since leaving Britain. I had not expected my first view of this fabled tropical island to be one of grey skies, sea and rain, I had thought it would be of sunshine, palm trees and colour. Reality was here and I had discovered that even tropical islands have their off-days.

Small boats buzzed between ships and shore resembling busy beetles as they ferried goods and people to and from the wharf. On the wharf itself brown-skinned, scantily clad men carrying loads upon their heads or backs transported goods to waiting lorries, while large, black, arrogant crows stalked among the bales and sacks prodding for pickings. Different scents pervaded our nostrils as we gazed about. From the shore came wafting on the air the smell of fresh vegetation, an aroma which had not been present for the past few weeks and which gave promise of new things to come. With the smell of greenery were mixed more exotic and musty perfumes we were as yet unable to identify.

The order was given to collect our belongings and muster on deck. Forming ranks, we awaited the next move. Long barge shaped boats were already along side the *Esperance Bay* being filled with baggage from the hold, swung over the side in large nets by the ship's derrick. As we watched our baggage go, a landing craft eased its way to the base of the steps attached to

156

the ship's side. Then came our turn to move. Making our way gingerly down the metal steps swaying slightly with the movement of the sea, we successfully negotiated the transfer into the landing craft, taking our last farewell of the *Esperance Bay* as we sped towards our first landfall for several weeks.

11

Stepping ashore was a milestone in my life, my first footing on a foreign shore. My adventure had truly begun. Everything was new and different; the mixture of sounds and smells which assailed our ears and nose; the sights which met our gaze; the town people with their burbling speech which seemed to roll off their tongues; the spicy aroma of the dock area; the people's dress; the large white buildings of the warehouses. As we stepped ashore the clouds rolled away and the sun appeared, dispersing the greyness of the rainfall, emphasising the colour of all around us. Reflecting from the white buildings light was introduced to the shabbiest of objects and even the big black crows shone as their feathers were touched by its radiance. The warmth generated released and increased further the perfumes pervading the air and at last I really felt that I had reached my expected tropical island.

With the sun and warmth came an increase in humidity which compelled us to remove our raincoats and caused beads of perspiration to form on our bodies. From the back of the naval truck which transported us on the next stage of our travel, we caught glimpses of the town. As we moved out of the dock area the warehouses were replaced by low open-fronted shops of ramshackle appearance filled with household goods, food and clothing for sale, most of the clothing being lengths of cloth with which to make saris or *dhotis*, the skirt-like garment worn by most of the men. Shopkeepers stood or squatted beside their displayed wares conversing with friends or awaiting customers. Loaded barrows were hauled by men bent between the double-shafted handles.

As we drove into the centre of the town the streets became

wider, as did the monsoon drains running along each side. The buildings became more substantial, two or three storeys in height, possessing doors and shuttered windows and some having shady colonnades to protect the interior from the sun's glare. Graceful women in brilliantly coloured saris strolled leisurely along the pavements bordering the buildings. Men wearing white *dhotis* or wide white slacks and white shirts went about their business between the commercial premises of banks, shops and administration. Rickshaw drivers ran carrying their passengers along the streets in the comparative coolness of early morning.

From the business centre of the town the truck drove through wide roads lined with arching trees bearing bright red blossom known as 'Flame of the Forest'. In these more spacious and quiet surroundings dwelt the families of the wealthier members of the community, in airy colonial style houses of copious dimensions, surrounded by large gardens contained within walls or railings and filled with shady trees and flowering shrubs. Colour and light were everywhere; on the sunlit white buildings; in the blue and now cloudless sky; sparkling on the ripples of the sea; in the trees and flowers and in the bright dresses and shining brown skins of the people themselves. It was a feast for the eyes after the drabness and austerity of wartime Britain and gave a delighted lift to my heart.

My attention was recalled to the truck which had now come to a halt before a tall pair of wrought-iron gates set in a high wall surrounding one of these grand houses. Two naval guards stood by the gate. After a check by one of them the truck entered a drive which stretched back a hundred yards or so to a large white mansion with red-tiled roof and overhanging wide balconies. Steps led to the imposing doorway, but we were not to enter there. Our vehicle stopped before a wooden building just inside the gates which we discovered to be the regulating office of the quarters. A petty officer took charge calling from a list of names of those to be accommodated in Kent House as we found it to be called. Eileen's name and mine were among those read out and we were glad to know we would remain together. Once we and our kit-bags were unloaded the truck went on its

W.R.N.S. QUARTERS AT KENT HOUSE, COLOMBO

way again to deposit others at different quarters around the area. A quick wave of farewell to our companions was all we had time for before we were rounded up by the petty officer who checked our details and handed us over to another Wren to direct us to our sleeping-quarters.

Any illusions of living in the grand style were soon dispelled. Long palm-thatched huts had been erected throughout the grounds, connected to one another by raised cement paths. Each hut was identified by a number, the only difference between them. The walls were built up to three quarters of the height to the eves, leaving a quarter of space open to the elements and protected only by the overhanging palm thatch. Open doorways without doors were screened by a small interior wall and in true naval fashion all were blancoed enough to blind one with their dazzling whiteness.

The interior of each *banda*, as the huts were named, was divided into two sections each housing seven Wrens. Each Wren was provided with a bed and beside it a locker or small cupboard in which to store personal belongings and at the end of the division was an area where clothes could be hung. The beds were draped with mosquito nets hung from the rafters in the roof. These not only helped to keep off the mosquitoes, but protected us from the multitude of other insects which fell from the thatch above us. The floor was of bare cement across which the occasional scorpion scuttled so it was not advisable to walk around with bare feet. I remembered a piece of advice my father had given me, learnt in his army days in the Middle East, and always turned my shoes upside down and tapped them sharply to shake out any lurking creepy-crawlies before putting them on. The *bandas* were sprayed at frequent intervals by brown men in green suits who wore masks and carried cylinders of DDT on their backs. This spraying with DDT kept mosquitoes and other insect pests at bay to a large extent and because of this, Colombo at this time was free of malaria. In spite of these precautions it was still necessary for us to have our daily intake of anti-malarial tablets which caused the skin of those who had been taking them for some time to take on a yellowish tinge. All forces' personnel were also issued with salt-tablets to combat loss of salt due to excessive sweating in the extremely humid climate.

After a month or two in Ceylon I discovered my hair to be noticeably thinner. It was also much lighter in colour. Luckily, I had arrived with a fairly thick head of hair, but my hair being very fine in texture did not adapt as well as some of my friends whose hair was more wiry in construction. One friend who arrived with strong but straight hair found the climate caused hers to become curly! The Sinhalese and Tamil women always appeared to have thick, strong and shiny black hair which I was told was kept that way due to the application of coconut-oil and which was almost always worn smoothed back from the face and tied into a traditional chignon on the back of the neck. This style of hairdressing looked most elegant and attractive, especially when decorated with a small garland of flowers for festive occasions.

On arrival at a new quarters, having found one's bed, the next priority is the geography of the rest of the new abode and particularly the whereabouts of the ablution facilities. In Kent House these were in separate blocks strategically placed within the radius of several dormitory *bandas*. Again, with thatched roofs and cement floors you ran the risk of sharing your bath or shower in the company of spiders, cockroaches or any one or more of a number of unspecified beetles all appearing to be of massive proportions! A careful inspection of the surroundings was advisable before indulging in the pleasure of the refreshing water.

In the heat and humidity of Ceylon's climate it was necessary to bathe and change several times a day in order to keep at bay the various skin complaints such as prickly-heat which the tropical climate activates. Another hurdle to be negotiated when going to the ablution block was to check it was not already occupied by one or more of the Tamil cleaners employed by the navy to maintain the premises. Due to the irregular hours of the twenty-four hour watch system we worked, there were always girls trying to get showers or baths throughout the day, but frequently finding the ablution block occupied by a male Tamil cleaner scrubbing or brushing the

162

building out with his besom broom ankle deep in water or cleaning round the basins in the leisurely fashion of those who live in tropical climes. It was annoying when one was rushing to get on duty or having come off duty was trying to prepare for an evening out. The only remedy was to find another ablution block in an adjacent group. I never quite understood why it was that while women cleaners were employed for the sleeping *bandas*, male cleaners were employed for the ablution blocks.

Bins and boxes for the disposal of rubbish and unwanted items were provided near each *banda* and became the picking ground of the large black scavenging crows which were prevalent on the island. They stalked the paths of our quarters keeping their beedy eyes open for an opportunity to snatch anything that took their fancy, strutting impudently at ease and moving to one side only at the last second before the human footfall. They never troubled to move far or fly away and no-one bothered them to do so.

Having spent my first night in the musty and enveloping folds of a mosquito net and eaten my breakfast in yet another long *banda*-type building, whose sides were enclosed with wire netting to prevent the crows from stealing the food from our plates, I received a message to report to regulating office. There I was told to be ready to take the transport in to HMS *Anderson* for the next watch and report to the Wren officer there. Wondering what was ahead of me, I did as instructed.

HMS *Anderson* turned out to be a signal station situated a few miles outside Colombo. Royal Marines guarded its gates and many straggling white buildings of mostly single-storey height occupied the interior area. These were joined by cement paths, the overhanging eves of the buildings providing shade from the brilliant sun. A WRENS third officer checked my name and details and then conducted me to one of these buildings. Inside it had the appearance of an office, with desks or tables on some of which stood typewriters and all the other implements such as pens, ink and paper that one would expect to see in any office in those days. No handy ball-point pens or word processors were available to us at that time. Sitting at the desks were three or four Wrens, some naval ratings, a naval leading hand and a young naval officer, all working quietly at their various tasks, while from the adjacent room came the muffled clatter of teleprinters.

As we walked in the young naval officer stood up greeting the WRNS officer. Returning the greeting Third Officer then turned to me and said, 'This is Sublieutenant Page. He will be your duty officer from now on.' In correct naval fashion I smartly executed a salute and waited for instructions. Third officer having completed the introductions left and Sublieutenant Page and I stood looking at one another. He asked a few questions about my previous work to which I answered, 'Yes, Sir' or 'No, Sir' as was necessary and as discipline decreed, when he suddenly said, 'Forget the "Sir" bit, call me Harry.' This shook me. Coming from the strictly run regime of Bletchley Park and its numerous surrounding Wren quarters, I had not yet become attuned to the much more friendly, relaxed atmosphere of the overseas station. To begin with I compromised by avoiding both name and rank altogether, but gradually as time went on I discovered everyone was on first name terms, apart that is when Wrens addressed WRNS officers and then I used the correct term 'Ma'am'.

Harry escorted me to an unoccupied desk and explained the method of signal distribution to which I was assigned. Once I had picked up the basic essentials of the job, with a friendly 'Ask me if you get stuck' or words to that effect, he returned to his desk. I settled down to my new work and to surveying those who were sharing in it.

Not everyone worked the twenty-four hour watch system as I was to do. Some members of the section worked day-watch only. Margo and Fugi were two Wrens in this watch along with some of the ratings. Apart from the hours of duty we never had any contact with one another. Wrens on the same watch might come from different quarters in different areas of Colombo and never meet except on duty.

The overall boss of our section was a Mr Bennett, a civilian who had been working with Cable and Wireless. He was a man of middle-age, or at least seemed so to me, a young girl of nineteen. His wife, a blonde lady who had a problem with her roll-ons, (an elasticated body belt to hold in one's figure) also worked at HMS *Anderson*. Without the stable anchorage of stockings to attach suspenders to, the roll-ons were inclined to slide upwards, which is why I remember Mrs Bennett mostly for the little wriggle she gave on rising from a sitting position, in an attempt to adjust the up-riding roll-ons.

Tubby, our leading hand, was a pleasant-faced man slightly older than most of the others and sat at a desk at the end of the room while Harry, as duty officer, had his desk in the middle of the room. As his nickname implies, Tubby was of slightly short and rotund stature and was blessed with a quiet humour. At the end of the war, back in England once more, I met him unexpectedly at a London underground station where he was working as an engineer on one of the lifts. Various other people wandered in and out during the watch in the course of their work, but I was never fully aware of their particular occupations. Any discourse they had was held with the watch officer or leading hand.

The twenty-four hour watch system meant working watches of six hours, duration, then six hours off duty to eat and sleep before starting a further six hours on watch. The only variation was the dog-watch from 16 00 to 20 00 hours, a period of four hours, after which we had just enough time to snatch a meal and get a few hours sleep before being shaken out of bed by the duty Wren in order to be on watch at 2 a.m. This was the time I disliked most of all. It was difficult enough to sleep at the best of times with all the activity and movement of Wrens preparing for duty, coming off duty or dressing up for their evening escorts. It seemed no sooner had one managed to settle down than you were dragged back into consciousness, or in my case semi-consciousness, required to dress in semi-darkness and compel your legs to take you to the waiting transport. It took the length of the journey and the jolting of the truck before I was fully aroused and ready for work.

During night-watch, which was usually a quiet period as far as work went, we were given a short break to visit the canteen and get something to eat and drink. I had not yet found my way around the station and was therefore quite pleased as well as surprised when the sublieutenant invited me to join him in the officers' canteen. The canteen boasted a few cane easy-chairs and such delicacies as coffee and baked beans on toast which can be surprisingly welcome in the middle of a night watch. Harry turned out to be cheerful and chatty, an amusing companion with a friendly disposition towards the human race in general. The short break over, we returned to the office and work, but in the quiet breaks Harry came to my desk to resume conversation. Having been abroad for some time, he was interested to hear what had been happening in Britain, what radio programmes were popular and what were the latest songs. It seemed that singing was his hobby also.

The following twenty-four hours was an off-duty period in which we were free to sleep, eat and catch up on our make and mend or take recreation. Eileen was working different watches from myself and was in another *banda*, as were other girls from the *Esperance Bay*. We managed to snatch a few words here and there, but had little chance to discuss our new situations. Post and messages were delivered to regulation office and on reporting in, 'Any mail or messages?' was a question everyone asked. Some girls had been stationed in Colombo for two or three years and felt very out of touch with home. Letters helped to ease the parting.

Servicewomen stationed abroad in the Far East were confined to quarters after 6 p.m. when darkness fell unless they had the protection of an escort. The escort was obliged to sign for the Wren or Waaf he was taking out for the evening, giving his name, number, rank and station or base. He was required to return his female by 10 p.m. unless she had a late pass which enabled her to remain out until 11.30 p.m., or a rare weekend pass which entitled her to spend the night in a suitably approved establishment such as the YWCA.

Those girls who were new arrivals and had no escort available were free to sign a list to attend a dance at a nearby naval, RAF or army station provided they were conducted there and back by official service transport. Since British females on the island were outnumbered by at least ten to one by the masses of British troops it did not take long for any girl to find an escort. In fact, the difficulty was to spend a quiet evening or afternoon in quarters in order to wash your hair or write letters. Invariably, some hopeful male would arrive at regulating office and want your company for an hour or two. It seemed that most girls had a string of beaux competing for their favours.

On the day following my first twenty-four hours' duty watch I was told there was a message for me in the regulating office. It was an invitation out for that evening and was signed 'Harry Page'. I was puzzled. I didn't remember anyone of that name. I decided to take the path of caution by phoning the number given and leaving a message regretting I was already committed for that evening. As it happened one of our ship board companions I had come to know arrived to take me out. It was not until my next spell on watch that it dawned on me who Harry Page was: the friendly young sublieutenant. Luckily my refusal was not held against me and the friendly atmosphere continued to exist.

My free time was used to explore Colombo town and its surrounding beaches. Those girls who had been there for some time passed on local information of places to visit and how to get there. Often a group of girls and men went together to beauty spots such as the well-known Mount Lavinia beach, a lovely sandy beach with rocky outcrops and backed by coconut palms and other greenery. It nevertheless had a darker side. The sea, though looking so blue and inviting, had a very strong undertow current and many swimmers found themselves unable to make their way back to the beach. Some fishermen of the area acted as lifeguards and risked their own lives to save many an unwary servicemen by leaping from rock to rock to endeavour to reach the swimmer in difficulties with his simple, but effective life-saving apparatus. This consisted of a long flexible bamboo cane on the end of which was a ring, again made from bamboo. The lifeguard would try to position the ring around the drowning person and haul him in to the shore. Many lives were saved by these men, but there were, regrettably, also many deaths. I was not a swimmer, but had walked along the edge of the sea and felt its strength, so although sun and water beckoned I decided to save my opportunity to learn to swim for the comparative safety of the swimming-pool.

Overlooking the beach was Mount Lavinia Hotel. Built in Colonial style, its white porticoes and verandahs stood on a small rocky peninsular and caught most of the cooler sea breezes. From its terraces one had an excellent view of a long stretch of beach and expanse of sea, or the few nearby shops selling ivory carvings and filergree silver work among other art and crafts of the island. The elephant was the symbol of Ceylon and ebony and ivory carved elephants were to be seen everywhere in all sizes from many tiny replicas hidden in nut-like shells to large wooden carvings two feet or more in height. They could be bought singularly or by the herd or, if one preferred, in an artistic arch following one another in diminishing size. I believe few service people came home from Ceylon without an elephant of some kind.

Lace work was a craft practised by some of the women of the island. In the cool tiled verandahs at Mount Lavinia Hotel and other favoured places in town, women could be seen working with nimble fingers at their lace pillows moving the many bobbins to form intricate patterns on the edgings, doilies and mats they made for sale.

The centre of town was some distance from Kent House. If one had an escort he usually arranged a taxi or rickshaw to travel into town, otherwise there were naval trucks driving in and out at regular times throughout the day. With other Wrens, or sometimes on my own, I travelled into town on one of these trucks which drove us most conveniently to the entrance of the forces' canteen where one could eat, drink, or relax in comfortable cane chairs. This canteen was a useful meeting place and not far from it was another notable rendezvous, the tall clock and lighthouse which stood on its arches in the middle of the main street. As a landmark or rendezvous it was impossible to miss as during the day its large clock reminded one of time passing and at night its light flashed its presence. There was no blackout in Colombo at this time as the Japanese had been driven back from any surrounding areas, so we were free to enjoy the benefit of artificial light. I loved to see the glow of the oil lamps and charcoal burners used by the local people, the small soft pools of light gleaming on men's dark skins as they worked at their task or craft in the slightly cooler temperature of a tropical evening. The charcoal and oil created a distinctive smoky yet smokeless aroma and, combined with the unhurried movements of the people, gave the night a dreamlike quality.

The shops and stalls of town were full of exotic and fascinating wonders: bright and beautiful saris delightfully embroidered in brilliant colours and designs, some of such fine material that it was possible to draw the whole six yards contained in each sari through a wedding ring without damaging the fabric; lovely jewellery, particularly sapphires and rubies which are mined in the island, and skillfully incorporated into necklaces, rings, earrings and other pieces to grace the body of some lucky women; intriguing, dainty, silver filigree work fashioned into butterfly and flower shapes to make delicate brooches and other ornaments. Most of my first pay-packet was spent on some of these delightful objects to send home as gifts.

Other wonders in this Aladdin's cave were the colourful local fruits. How marvellous it was after so many years of rationing and absence of such goodies to be able to indulge in bananas, melons and numerous new varieties of delicious fruits such as mangos and pawpaw, unknown to me previously. Sweet things also were in abundance. A regular visitor to our quarters was a Sinhalese man who came on his bicycle, strapped to which was a box containing large rectangles of pink and white coconut ice, sweet and cool to the taste. How wonderful to be free to buy without coupons or restriction! Tea, coffee, meat, materials; in fact, almost everything which was in such short supply in Britain was available for a few rupees. It was indeed a wonderland.

The Pettah, which is the market place or bazaar area of Colombo, was a fascinating place to visit, although one was advised against going there alone. It was considered a red-light district by naval authorities who certainly did not approve of a member of the WRNS frequenting such a place. At times there were outbreaks of cholera and the whole area was put out of

169

bounds. However, Harry and I went on one or two occasions to a local restaurant named Pilawis, where we would dine in little cubicles with wooden tables and bench seats and pick at a whole roasted chicken with our fingers. I cannot remember having anything except a whole chicken each, no vegetables or other side-dishes, but the whole chicken was only about the size of a pigeon, so we were not as greedy as it sounds.

At other times I joined Harry for evening dinner at the guest-house where he and a number of other naval officers were billeted along with some European civilians who were working with the services. The guest-house was run by a Mrs Terry, an English woman who had lived for many years in Ceylon. It was here that I tasted my first curry, an eye-watering experience. Curries, like a number of other exotic dishes, need a gentle approach, and gradually I acquired a taste for the milder variety. One of the points to remember was not to drink cold water until *after* you had finished eating or it would prolong the agony!

A dish that appeared often on the menu at Mrs Terry's establishment was rabbit. This puzzled me a little as I could not remember seeing or hearing of rabbits as part of the fauna of Ceylon. It was not until we took an impromptu walk around the back garden one evening and found cages upon cages of cats and kittens of all shapes and sizes, that I realised from whence the 'rabbits' came. No doubt 'rabbit' was also an ingredient in the Sunday curries we had been enjoying!

The coffee made in Ceylon with goats-milk and plenty of sweetening was delicious, particularly after a late duty watch when one was feeling a little jaded. Sometimes we stopped at a wayside coffee shop where the shopkeeper would pour the hot coffee from one container into another held a little distance away until a foaming froth developed. Sitting in the transport sipping this nectar soon restored our spirits and I have yet to taste anything to better it.

Our white uniforms, which required frequent washing, we took to the *dobhi* man to launder. He was very conveniently situated just beside the gates of Kent House and lines of white skirts were to be seen spread on the grass to dry in the hot sunshine. Unfortunately, the grass adjoined the pathway used by the populace, many of whom indulged in the habit of chewing betel nut. This stained the insides of their mouths a bright red from the juice which they spat haphazardly on roads and paths. My skirt was returned one day with one of these stains marking the front and had to be discarded as the stain was almost impossible to remove.

Among the seemingly hundreds of girls stationed in Kent House, I was surprised to find another girl from our village. Paula had gone out on a slightly earlier draft and although we managed to meet up once or twice we did not know one another very well and our varying duties did not provide much opportunity to improve our acquaintance. We did, however, meet up again on our return home.

Another unexpected meeting occurred when I was walking along Mount Lavinia beach with some friends. There was a sudden shout of 'Gwen?' from the sea. From the waves arose a boy from my brother's school. 'What are you doing here?' was his question. Bill it seemed was in the Fleet Air Arm and his ship was in port for a time. Again, it was a fleeting meeting as he had to rejoin his ship and I could not easily leave my friends, but contacts like that seemed to make home less far away.

On 6 August 1945 the Allies dropped their secret weapon. The fearful first atomic bomb was dropped on the town of Hiroshima in the islands of Japan. On 9 August 1945 a second atomic bomb was dropped on the town of Nagasaki. The resulting horrendous devastation will never be forgotten. On 14 August 1945 the Emperor of Japan broadcast on radio the unconditional surrender of his country. On 15 August 1945 Japan surrendered formally to the Allies. At last the war was truly over!

Again, I cannot remember any unbridled rejoicing, I think it was mainly a great relief that there was to be no more bombing and killing, but at last life could return to normal, although, of course, after six years few could remember what normal might be. There was much to be done before we could resume an unrestricted or comfortable form of living, but at least we could now start to work towards it.

171

Victory was celebrated a few days later by a large parade of representatives of the armed forces and other services which took place along the sea front close to the Galle Face Hotel. The salute was taken by Lord Louis Mountbatten who was the supreme commander of the south-east Asian command. Because of my lack of height (I am only five feet one inch) I was not picked to take part in the parade so had the pleasure of avoiding the necessary rehearsal drills. Only those girls of the required measurement were obliged to become part of the parade to represent the WRNS in the victory march.

Other more relaxed and social functions were arranged by the town and every forces' station to celebrate the occasion, but as far as I remember all celebrations were fairly restrained. Most people were just glad to know that hostilities were finally to cease.

One of the nearby RAF stations decided to hold a dance in the sergeants' mess on the evening of VJ Day and notices to this effect were posted on the boards of all the WRNS quarters in the vicinity. I happened to be off-duty that evening and had not arranged to do anything else so put my name on the list to attend. When the RAF truck arrived, I climbed aboard to find only one other girl on it. I was rather surprised, but hoped that others might be picked up from other quarters. Reaching the sergeants' mess, we walked in and found we were indeed the only two girls they had managed to recruit, and there were more than a dozen sergeants all expectantly waiting and eager to dance. So overwhelmed were we by their attentions that eventually a senior NCO took charge and allowed each man two turns around the floor at a time before we changed partners for the next in the queue. By the time the transport came to take us back to quarters we and our overworked feet were exhausted. We certainly felt we had done our bit towards celebrating VJ night.

The usual mode of transport in our off-duty time with escorts was either by rickshaw or taxi. The rickshaw was the more exciting. They were single seats with a pram-like folding hood, finely balanced on two large but narrow-rimmed wheels. Attached to the chassis were two long, slender wooden shafts between which the rickshaw man stood, gripping a shaft in each hand. When given your destination, he set off at a rhythmic trot, weaving in and out of the mixed traffic of cars, bicycles and bullock carts, keeping up a steady pace until you came to the named place. Then the shafts were set down, the sweat wiped from his brow with the cloth tied around his neck and his hand held out for the fare. It was wise to have agreed how much it was to be beforehand.

The sensations experienced by the passenger while being bowled along in this way, were, on the whole, pleasant. The breeze engendered by the movement was cooling to one's body in the great humidity of that climate and the movement relaxing, provided one kept one's eyes closed against the hair-raising activities of the other vehicles. The rickshaw men were a breed of lean and wiry men, with not an ounce of surplus fat on them. The rivalry among them for passengers was great and it was usually necessary to pick one rickshaw quickly from the selection offered, or you found yourself continually pestered and disagreements amongst the rickshaw runners noisy and voracious.

However, there came a time when I would have been glad to have seen so many and when they were notable by their absence. A friend in the Fleet Air Arm was in Colombo for a few days' leave from his ship. He had asked me to partner him to a dance at Colombo Town Hall, an imposing building situated some way out of the main town area in a pleasant tree-lined road and surrounded by wide green lawns. We had an enjoyable evening until it was time for me to return to quarters. When leaving the town hall we walked into a monsoon deluge. There was not a taxi in sight and it was essential for me to report back on time or we should both be in trouble. We decided to start walking in the hope that we might find a taxi in another street. Within seconds we were both thoroughly wet through and although we walked for some distance there were still no taxis to be had. Feeling like a couple of drowned rats, with my hair having lost any pretence to curl, my friend suddenly espied a lone rickshaw man sheltering under a large tree. With the aid of a pocketful of money my friend persuaded him to carry us both back to quarters in his one rickshaw. It is the only time I have travelled in a rickshaw *à deux*. The runner deserved every cent of his money, and although we were still late there was an understanding petty officer on duty who took one look at the water dripping from my hair, nose and sodden clothes and forgave me.

Another form of transport I tried for the very first time was pillion-riding on a motor cycle. A chief petty officer friend of mine borrowed a motorbike and suggested that we should go and take a look at Bentota, a picturesque lagoon some thirty miles or more from Colombo. Eager to see as much as possible of this beautiful island, I agreed. It was not until he arrived with the bike that I realised how awkward it was to ride astride in the rather tight skirt of the WRNS uniform. Hoping not to be recognised and with chinstrap firmly fixed, (no safety helmets in those days) we set off. All went well for the first twenty miles or so and then the engine began to emit strange splutterings and noises. My friend became concerned and we dismounted. To our horror, flames began to spurt from the engine. Hurriedly, we sought to smother them with dust from the road. Luckily, this put out the fire, but left us with an engine choked with dust. Jack tinkered with the engine to try and clear it, while I exchanged smiles with the group of interested children who had gradually gathered around us. Jack managed to clean some of the dust away and decided to try to start the engine. It sprang into life and he shot away up the road leaving me standing in the middle of a Sinhalese village surrounded by shy, giggling children and eyed more suspiciously from a distance by their curious parents.

I assumed Jack would be returning for me, so took the opportunity to look around at the bamboo and palm thatch houses, the chickens and goats wandering between them and the children with their beautiful big brown eyes. Five or ten minutes passed and still no sign of my friend. It was then I heard an engine coming up the road, not Jack, but a naval truck with half-a-dozen 'Jacks' aboard. The driver put on his brakes sharply when he saw me standing by the roadside.

'Hey Jenny, what are you doing out here?' was his greeting.

Explaining what had occurred, I was invited to jump aboard and we set off to find out what had happened to Jack. Half a mile or so further on we found him. The engine had conked out once again and he was trying vainly to restart it. He was beginning to make progress, so I thanked my rescuers and said I would take my chances with Jack and the motor-bike and waved them farewell. Eventually the engine was running smoothly once more, but by this time it was too late to get to Bentota and we drove instead to a nearer beach and rest-house where we relaxed in the shade of some palm-trees for an hour or so before making our, I am glad to say, uneventful journey back.

Another way to explore the island was by hitching lifts on naval transports which were continually travelling between naval stations. It was helpful if you had a friend 'in the know'. In this way Harry and I saw Galle, a town on the southern point of Ceylon, fortified by the Portuguese, captured by the Dutch and again by the British. Its high grassy slopes still retained the ruins of the old stone walls and buildings mellowed and romanticised by time. Away from the busier areas of the town, all was peace and tranquillity, the old grey stones, the fresh green grassy slopes, the absolutely clear turquoise sea twenty feet or so below us, the blue sky above and waving coconut palms within view along the shore. It was the perfect setting for a romantic novel. Our only companions were the goats who kneeling on their forelegs, grazed on the grass, cropped smooth by their efforts, and the silent colourful fish in the transparent water which lapped against the ancient walls.

While we sat in silence enjoying the beauty around us, a black shape came out of some bushes close by, ran swiftly and silently up the bank and disappeared into the ruins. It happened so quickly that I was unable to distinguish very clearly, but it moved like a cat and had a long tail although it was far bigger than any domestic cat I had ever seen. Could it have been a black panther? I shall never be really sure.

On 25 August 1945 I was invited to join Harry and some friends for a Victory gala celebration at the Silver Faun, a nightclub of which Harry was a member. It was a popular and

175

selectively decorous establishment patronised by the better-off members of the resident population and a few lucky European officers. It was a new experience for me and a chance to dress up. Long evening-dress was required. I felt my one and only long dress was a little too immature for such a sophisticated venue, but I could not afford to buy a new one. I pondered over the problem with some of my room-mates. One came up with a suggestion. She had a heavy silk-textured negligee in a pretty shade of blue, the form-fitting V-necked bodice of which was fastened with small buttons covered in the same material. If I sewed up the skirt it would make a reasonable evening dress. When I tried it on it was a perfect fit and hung beautifully in folds around my body with plenty of allowance for dancing. We agreed a price and I set to work.

When I dressed for my evening out, I was quite pleased with the resulting effect. Larry, my escort for the evening, duly arrived with Harry and Midge and we took a taxi to The Silver Faun. Larry, another young sublieutenant watch officer, looked slim and elegant in his naval evening mess-jacket and trousers, 'mess undress' I believe it was termed, or 'monkey-jacket and cummerbund' as most young officers called it. Midge was a Wren like myself also enjoying a chance to dress up. It was my first meeting with Larry and Midge and I was pleased to discover them both pleasant companions.

Coming from a chapel-going, teetotal background, night-clubs were a new venture for me and I am not quite sure what I expected. What I found was an attractive building containing a good sized sunken dance floor surrounded by colonnades raised a foot or so above the dance floor level, in which stood tables and chairs. All the tables were attractively laid with white clothes and decorated with bright flowers. Around these tables sat the members and their guests, the men in tropical white evening-suits making a perfect background to the ladies' brilliantly coloured and embroidered saris. I was captivated by the loveliness of some of these beautiful garments. As they danced to the western tunes of waltz, foxtrot or quickstep played by the musicians on a dias at one end of the room, the delicate fabric of these graceful robes flowed about them displaying the gold or silver embroidered borders which glinted as they caught the light from the lamps above. Almost all the Sinhalese women here wore their hair in the traditional drawn-back style, black and sleek, the severeness relieved by a circlet of flowers around the dark coil on their necks. Tamil and Sinhalese waiters dressed in scrupulously white *dhoti* skirts and tunics served the tables under the supervision and overall charge of an older Sinhalese man who wore his long greying hair high on his head, secured by a crescent-shaped tortoishell comb. The comb denoted his higher caste, evidence that he and his kind carried no burdens upon their head, the normal way of carrying goods for the lower caste Sinhalese. Other attendants came to the tables carrying trays of flowers, orchids and exotically scented frangipani. These were formed into sprays to decorate the ladies' dresses or hair.

The menu consisted entirely of European food varying from Seer fish and Russian salad, stuffed roast duck with green peas, roast lamb and mint sauce, to a supper dish of sausage and mash or bacon and eggs. Hardly exciting for us, but at least different for the Sinhalese customers. The wine-list printed on the back of the menu and programme which I still have, gives a choice of whisky, brandy, gin, cocktails, victory cup (wine), sherry, port and white wine. My escort was a little surprised, but very understanding when I opted for fresh lime juice. In fact, I remained teetotal throughout my WRNS service and enjoyed myself in spite of (or because of) it. Wrens were issued with two bottles of beer per week whilst in the tropics, presumably on account of the heat, but I always gave mine to the matelots on the gate.

As it was a special night we were treated to a Victory celebration cabaret as follows:

10 p.m.		Ballroom Formation
		Mrs Wijeratne, Mrs de Soysa,
		Mrs David, Miss Ranasingne,
		Messrs Wijeratne, Souza,
		Amerasinghe, Krisnaratne.
11 p.m.	a)	Naval Manoeuvre

177

<pre>
                  Nancy Mary Fenton
       b)   Café de Paris
                  Joe Pelly Fry
                  Ruth Squieres
       c)   Blues on Broadway
                  (By special request)
                  Yvonne Bradley
11.45 p.m. a)   Scotland for Aye
                  Yvonne Bradley
       b)   America will be there
                  Jo Pelly Fry
                  Nancy Mary Fenton
                  Ruth Squieres
       c)   Britannia
                  Virginia Pelly Fry
</pre>

A footnote remarks:

> 'The grateful thanks of all members are due to Miss
> Bradley and to all the Artistes for having rendered
> the Club so much gratuitous service.'

To be able to enjoy the entire cabaret it was necessary for me to obtain a weekend pass and book a room at the YWCA. It was a delightful evening. Our partners were both good dancers, Larry performed an excellent old-fashioned or Viennese waltz, and both men were attentive escorts. The atmosphere was happy, friendly, but always eminently respectable. My parents had no cause to worry. By midnight the show was over, the dancing finished. Larry hired a taxi and bade me goodnight outside the YWCA.

My room in the hostel was attractively decorated with floral patterned curtains and bedcover and I was soon settled in its comfortable bed. After a good night's rest I was awoken in the morning by the houseboy tapping on the door. At my answer he entered carrying a breakfast tray holding a welcome cup of tea and a plate of delicious looking fruit. What a welcome change it was from the dull breakfast at quarters where I would certainly not be served breakfast in bed!

All too soon this luxurious life was over and I was back to work and quarters once more, but my second-hand negligee-cum-evening-dress had seen me through and even brought flattering comments on my appearance, so all was well.

Although we continued to work our duties, there was little to do as what signals there were, were no longer in code. The first thing the Allied armies did was to free those who had been imprisoned by the Japanese. On 5 September British forces re-entered Singapore, releasing and re-patriating those who had been imprisoned in Changi jail. As the Allies made their way up-country more camps were found where prisoners had been confined in disastrous conditions. They too were released and transported to Singapore where they were embarked on ships which would return them to Britain. Colombo was a staging-post on their journey home where the ships docked for a few hours. I along with other Wrens went to the receiving centre at Eschelon Barracks near the sea-front to help where I could. We saw many sadly treated and sick men and heard some dreadful accounts of their privations. We also heard some of their worries about returning home, for most of these men had been prisoners and out of contact with home and families for four years. On one occasion I walked into Eshelon barracks and found a group of five soldiers, lean, wiry and very deeply tanned, standing in the drive and looking rather lost. I said to them, 'Hello, have you just arrived?' they simply stood and stared at me without answering. I tried again. 'Have you just come off the ship from Singapore?' At last one of them answered. Yes they had; and they all continued to stare at me.

Eventually my efforts achieved results, the ice was broken and I took them on a short guided tour of the town centre as they had seen nothing of Colombo but the docks until then. We finished our tour in the nearby forces' canteen where I treated them to a snack as none of them had been given any money so far. They ate very little, but talked much. It was as though the barriers had opened and I had great difficulty in keeping up with their questions.

For four years they had been prisoners of war and undergone extremely harsh treatment. The five I had befriended had been

179

made to work on the infamous Siam railway the enemy had forced them to build. They knew nothing of present-day happenings. What was my uniform they asked, and why did I address the women whose table we shared as Ma'am? When I explained that she was an officer they nearly exploded with their disbelief. Women officers?! They had never heard of such a thing! So I had to enrol the help of the WRNS officer to explain the role of the women's services to them. Of course, they also wanted to know about England, they were all English, and what damage had been done by the bombing. Did I know their town? Would people welcome them home? Their self-confidence and morale had undergone a tremendous battering. Their captors had told them that no woman would ever talk to them again. This was the reason they looked so taken aback when I first stopped to say hello. I hope I was able to allay some of their fears and make their meetings with their families a little easier.

When it was time for me to return to duty, I directed them back to the reception centre and went to wait for my transport. One of the men insisted upon waiting with me to see me safely on my way before he returned. Their ship sailed that evening and I never saw them again, but I hope they found happiness on their arrival in England to make up for those four long years.

In great contrast to these men were the visitors from the fleet of the USA. They came on a 'goodwill' visit for two days, all six thousand of them! The fleet consisted of two battleships, two destroyers and various other supporting vessels. Before the ships had put in to harbour the telephones in every WRNS quarter of Colombo were swamped with calls from women-hungry sailors trying to make a date with a girl, any girl as long as she was female, for their day in port. I say day and not days, for in their wisdom the commanders of the fleet had decided that the town would not be able to take an influx of six thousand men at one go and cut the number by allowing three thousand ashore the first day and another three thousand the second day. Since, as far as the servicemen already on the island were concerned, women were in short supply, this was a sensible move. Nevertheless, three thousand more men could only cause havoc in such a situation. Telephones in WRNS offices were taken off the hook, the Regulating Petty Officers in charge having become disgruntled and exasperated with the constant requests from voices with transatlantic accents for feminine company. Girls off duty, shopping in town, relaxing on the beach or even walking in the quieter residential roads, would find themselves accosted by desperate sailors. A friend and I were returning from an errand along a tree-lined avenue, peaceful and alone when a taxi appeared and came to an abrupt halt beside us. Four young sailors in US uniform tumbled out and stopped us. They were very polite in their approach and we were not offended, however, since we were both due to go on duty we could not accept their offer of company for the day, and no, we were sorry we did not know of any friends who would be free to join them. Our refusal was accepted with regret and resignation and we returned to our quarters while they piled back into their taxi to continue their search.

On our return from a four hour duty watch we dismounted from our naval transport at the gates of Kent House to find them besieged by American sailors still hopeful of finding a girl willing to spend a few hours with them. We entered the gates guarded by two British sailors armed with truncheons, to the calls of, 'Hi there', 'How are you?' 'What's your name?' 'What are you doing tonight?' from several different voices, and made our way through with a smile and a wave.

Later that evening, emboldened by a drink or two, some sailors broke into one WRNS quarter and ran through some of the *bandas* before being rounded up and ejected by the guards. The next day the guards were issued with rifles. The 'Snow-drops', US military police, called 'Snowdrops' because of the white helmets they wore, were out in force and girls did not go out without an escort. When the two days were up the fleet sailed away and life returned to normal once again, or put in naval terms, a calm sea and even keel.

12

After all prisoners of war had been returned, the war office decided it was the turn of servicewomen. I was able to stay in Ceylon until just before Christmas when I found my name on the draft list outside regulating office. I was not in a hurry to go home. I loved being in Ceylon, there was still much to see and do. Also Harry and I had fallen in love and become engaged to be married (but that is another story!) In the few months I had there we managed to explore some of the island, both along its coast and in the beautiful central hill area, and it was with deep regret that I embarked upon the *Nea Helles*, the ship that was to take me away from the warmth and sunshine back to the icy cold of a January in Scotland.

Apart from the returning forces personnel, the ship carried families of civilians returning to the United Kingdom, also wives and children of servicemen who had married while stationed in Ceylon. I wondered what some of the young Eurasian wives would make of England and its chilly and temperamental climate after the sunny, humid yet predictable temperatures of their own country. There were six girls in our cabin, all having a bunk each, but a friend was put into a cabin shared by five with one having to sleep on the floor.

We sailed on 21 December at five o'clock in the afternoon on a smooth sea. Just before we left Colombo, Radio SEAC people came aboard to take messages to relay to those left behind. The programme was also relayed throughout the ship. When my message to Harry saying I hoped he would soon follow was mentioned, the amazed voices of half a dozen girls could be heard to echo '*Harry Page!*' which gave me cause to wonder!

A choir was formed which I joined and a practice held each

morning. I enjoyed having something to do on what I knew was going to be a long voyage. In the evening the marines started a sing-song on the well deck below us. I quote from my letter to Harry:

'There were several Wrens, officers and a few civilians listening from the "gallery" as the marines called it. Just before the sing-song broke up for the night, they asked the "gallery" to oblige with a song. One of the fellows volunteered to render "Nellie Dean". He was loudly applauded and the others were hissed. Then they asked for a Wren to give voice, so I obliged with "When Irish Eyes Are Smiling". They seemed to like it and now they have nicknamed me The Colleen.'

The following evening the choir gave a carol concert which helped towards promoting something of the Christmas spirit in what was for us unusual circumstances. Later girls in my cabin said that the marines were calling for me to sing again. So the following night I returned to the 'gallery' and sang the 'Rose of Tralee.'

'They have one fellow there,' I wrote 'who makes a wonderful MC and comedian. He keeps everyone in fits of laughter. They have quite an audience of officers and Wrens listening to them now.'
'December 25 Christmas Day. Merry Christmas, darling. We were given a terrific breakfast this morning, porridge, kippers, bacon and eggs, bread, butter and marmalade and tea or coffee. I had to miss out on the bacon and egg, I couldn't take it!. . . The Marines on the deck below staged some boxing bouts and they got two of the small boy passengers of about nine years of age to box one another. The small boys thoroughly enjoyed themselves and so without a doubt did the spectators.'

At dinner we had turkey and Christmas pudding as tradition decrees and also a piece of Christmas cake. In the evening a dance was held on deck.

> 'It wasn't bad, except that when the ship rolled everyone was flung over to one side,' was my comment.

On 27 December we reached Aden, a short stop for refuelling only. In the harbour were two destroyers flying their paying-off pennants, adding colour to the generally stark background of this barren land. We were followed into harbour by an aircraft-carrier which dwarfed the destroyers.

The *Nea Helles* left Aden about five p.m., HMS *Howe* having left a couple of hours before us. That evening when the sing-song began we were once more on our way home. Again I was asked to sing and this time I did so from the well-deck. My singing had become a regular feature now. There was also a male singer, a soldier who had a beautiful tenor voice. I believe his name was Ben Baron. When he sang 'Jerusalem' all these hard-bitten marines remained hushed and absorbed as his voice soared into the clear night air.

On 28 December we sighted a high mountain on the starboard side, and we were back in the Red Sea.

> 'This evening I sang for the men again. They had asked me the previous evening to sing "I'll Take You Home Again, Kathleen" but I had not been able to remember the words. I thought them out afterwards and managed to remember the first verse, so I sang that and "Believe Me If All Those Endearing Young Charms". It is amazing how much these tough brawny men like these old sentimental songs.'

The Red Sea was still hot, but not nearly as hot as it had been on our outward journey, for which I was thankful. On Sunday 30 December it had cooled so much that rig of the day was bell-bottoms, tropical shirts, blue jackets and black shoes. For the first time we were provided with warm blankets for our bunks. The church service that morning was held in the first-class saloon and, being in the choir, I of course attended.

31 December, New Year's Eve. A dance was held on main deck and the marines organised a concert of their own on the deck below.

> 'At midnight everybody stopped dancing and the kissing commenced.'

With so few women on board we Wrens were in great demand, all in the spirit of New Year.

Of the return journey the one incident that stands out in my memory is of sailing through the Suez Canal on New Year's Eve on a ship crewed almost entirely by Scotsmen. Many of the Royal Marine passengers were also Scots on their way home and their jubilations could not go unnoticed. As we passed along the length of the canal, sirens blasting, men came tumbling out of the doors of suddenly lighted cabins where they had been peacefully sleeping, hurriedly pulling on their trousers as they did so, to see what all the noise was about. They probably thought that hostilities had recommenced. Instead, they were greeted with the sight of our liner with lights ablaze and the rails and deck crowded with madmen shouting at them. The fact that they were being wished a 'Happy New Year' may or may not have been understood. About twenty minutes past twelve pipes were blown to clear the decks and all service personnel retired to their cabins. Not so the crew. To continue the celebrations some members of the crew had sets of bagpipes which they played up and down the gangways of the ship until two in the morning. Altogether it was a memorable New Year's Eve!

New Year's Day 1946 found us in Port Said. As soon as people appeared on deck the bum-boats came to barter. Some people managed to buy handbags and other goods. A marine bought some oranges for me before the crew brought out the hoses to clear the decks to get the ship on her way. As we sailed through the Mediterranean Sea I chatted to one of the merchant navy officers who knew my brother's ship the SS *Beckenham*. It had been in convoy with them several times on Russian convoys.

Long voyages can be extremely tedious and I was glad to fill in time as duty Wren, taking my turns to clean our cabin, practising for the choir, rehearsing for the concert, whist-drives and, when I had nothing else to do, playing table-tennis with the two ratings acting as librarians on board. Not many people seemed to know that the table-tennis was available, so we were able to play several good games.

With the much cooler weather the sing-songs on deck ceased and instead film shows were provided in the recreation rooms. Some other Wrens and myself managed, with the connivance of the sublieutenant in charge, to sneak into some of the film shows held for the men. We had to shut our ears to some good-natured comments, but no one resented our presence. One of the films we watched was 'Follow the Boys' in which George Raft starred. I was much impressed by the way he wobbled his knees when dancing a jive! Another film starred my favourite Deanna Durbin in 'Hers to Hold', a third film showed Charles Boyer and Ingrid Bergman in 'Murder in Thornton Square'. Another thriller was 'Hanover Square'. The lads were not slow in showing their reactions to certain love scenes or to some of the more effeminate male singers in some of the short films shown. Their remarks caused us to laugh or blush in turn. It was just as well the lights were out.

A number of Wrens had obtained some SEAC shoulder-flashes which they sewed onto their blue jackets ready to impress the folks at home.

About 4 January we ran into rougher weather which caused the ship to roll a great deal. A dance was held in the troops' recreation room, but it was almost impossible to dance. If we managed to stand at all, as soon as the next wave struck the ship's side, all found themselves sliding across the floor to the opposite side willy-nilly. We did not get much dancing, but we had a lot of laughs.

Among the passengers returning on the *Nea Helles* was a London theatre producer. He was one of the organisers of the ship's concert in which I was asked to sing, but this time instead of the open deck the concert was held in one of the commodious recreation rooms of the pre-war liner.

With the change in the weather came a bout of feverish colds and a virus causing a mild form of dysentery. I managed to avoid the dysentery virus, but started a cold the day before the concert was due to take place. On 5 January, the day of the concert, it was much worse and I went down to sick-bay. Nurse was very sympathetic and gave me a dose of quinine and an inhalation. The quinine made me feel dizzy and light-headed, my legs seemed to be turned to jelly and I wanted to burst out crying for no particular reason. Nurse had me repeat the treatment four times that day and by the evening when the concert took place I just about managed to get through my four songs. The second evening, in spite of the ministrations of my sympathetic nurse, I had to drop out of the performance. Nurse and I persevered and with further doses of quinine, nasal drops and inhalations I was able to take part in the third, fourth and fifth performances although still weak at the knees. The show was a great success, with hearty laughs in all the right places and lots of appreciation afterwards.

On 10 January we entered the River Clyde and saw the smooth grey green hills of Scotland. As we sailed towards Greenock, tucked among the folds of the hills, we could see the grey stone houses closed against the winter's cold, bleak and unwelcoming. My thoughts flew back to the sunshine and colour I had left in Ceylon and I wondered if I should ever see that lovely island again. Not everyone felt as I did. There were many Scots on board among the marines to whom this landscape meant home, friends and happiness and eagerly they lined the rails to renew recognition of each familiar landmark. Signs of habitation increased as we came closer to the port of Greenock and excitement mounted. As the ship docked it was time to say goodbye to shipboard companions. For once more we had to separate in to our various squads to prepare for disembarkation and another journey, this time by rail, to take us to our home naval bases, the WRNS destination being Chatham barracks in Kent.

On 11 January we boarded the long train that was to take us south. The Wrens were consigned to the front carriage of the train which was to prove a disadvantage to us. Leaving Greenock at 7.30 a.m., our next stop was some hours later at Crewe. As the train slowed and pulled into Crewe Station we saw trestle tables loaded with sandwiches and other food behind which stood the motherly members of the WVS.

When the train pulled in, due to its extensive length the Wrens found themselves at the far end of the platform and by the time we had walked back to where the WVS ladies were serving, most of the food had disappeared into the hands of the sailors and marines lucky enough to have been consigned to the centre carriages. Also no-one had warned us to provide ourselves with a drinking utensil and although there were urns of tea there were not enough cups to go round, so we had no means of drinking. When the WVS ladies realised the situation they set to to provide more sandwiches for the by now very hungry girls. As I stood waiting, possibly looking a trifle forlorn, a marine called out, 'Hi Paddy, what's wrong?' (I was nicknamed Paddy because of the Irish songs I sang when on board ship.) 'Only that you lot have swiped all the food and left nothing for us!' was my reply. 'Can't have that' he said. 'Come here, we'll find some for you,' and they certainly did. I returned to my compartment with my arms laden with sandwiches and apples donated by the men, which I shared amongst the other girls there. My singing on board had paid off for although I did not know most of the men, they had recognised me.

With the addition of the extra sandwiches cut by the WVS ladies and the acquisition of a mug, we managed to survive the seventeen hour long tedious journey to Chatham. At Chatham Barracks we were allotted bunks in the spartan rooms of the Victorian (or older) brick buildings, unwarmed and un-friendly, where shivering and still hungry we tried to sleep. My recollections of Chatham are grey, not with the mist of time, but with cold, fog, frost and general cheerlessness. As we wrapped our bodies in extra vests, with another around the feet to detract from the iciness of the sheets and piled our overcoats on the bed, I for one wished I was back in the warm and

AND WHEN WE GOT THERE THE TABLE WAS BARE

189

colourful land of Ceylon. Luckily, our initial stay at Chatham was short. Once we had been checked in sick-bay for any unwelcome bugs, complied with the necessary paper work and collected our luggage from the barracks, we were taken in trucks to the railway station. There we had to unload from the trucks and reload all our baggage onto the train for Victoria, London. Thus we were sent home on leave, our final leave before our demobilisation.

It was good to see my family and home once more. Cindy was now a fourteen year old, the age I had been at the outbreak of war, and was travelling to school in St Albans each day. Mother and Dad looked worn and tired from the stresses and strains of the last six years for although hostilities had ended and there were no more air-raids to worry them, rationing and shortages still remained, if anything, tighter than they had ever been. They were to continue so for many more years yet and it was well into the 1950s before Britain was able to dispense with many of these restrictions.

I was badly in need of warm civilian clothes. Arriving in the middle of an English winter proved too much of a shock to the system and I found it almost impossible to keep warm. I wrote:

'It was so cold yesterday morning that I borrowed some coupons from Mother and Cindy and rushed down the street to try and buy a jumper. I managed to get a blue one in real wool and handknitted, but it cost me the fearful price of two pounds, ten shillings. It is a lovely thing and should keep me warm, but what a terrible price to have to pay! The utility jumpers only cost about fourteen shillings, but they are made of split wool and have very little warmth. . . . When I get my coupons I must buy myself an overcoat. One can buy utility coats from about three pounds upwards, but they don't look very warm for winter, also they are only half-lined for fifteen coupons. The better ones cost about fourteen or fifteen pounds and eighteen coupons.'

190

Housing too was desperately short. All furniture apart from second-hand items, which were quickly snapped up, was on dockets and in short supply. I could see that Harry and I were going to have a difficult time setting up home and would greatly miss the abundance and freedom we had had in Ceylon.

Something that had altered was the political situation. There had been a national general election in Britain on July 26 1945 when the Labour Party had a resounding victory. Churchill resigned and Clement Attlee became prime minister. The mood of the people had changed and was directed towards a time of peace and a better way of living for the majority of the population with a fairer share of the privileges of those in the higher echelons of society.

During my leave I received an unexpected telephone call. It was from Harry. I could not believe he was in England already. He told me he had flown home on compassionate grounds as his father had just died. I was sorry to hear the reason, but delighted to know I would soon see him again. We arranged to meet on St Pancras Station the next day. Harry almost failed to recognise me in my thick navy blue uniform with shirt, tie, heavy greatcoat and woollen gloves, so bundled up against the cold. The last time he had seen me I had worn the white, light uniform of the tropics.

Together we travelled to my home where he was introduced to the family for the first time. There was a certain amount of constraint on my family's part towards this unknown stranger, as they were all very fond of Gerry and had expected that he and I would eventually marry. In time they came to accept my choice and appreciate Harry's qualities. One year after we first met we were married in the Baptist church of my home village, to start a new and hopefully peaceful life together.

A Wartime Prayer for WRNS

Almighty God, who art ever the protector of those who go down to the sea in ships; bless we beseech Thee, the members of the Women's Royal Naval Service, who go forth to help of their brethren of the Royal Navy. Inspire them with the splendour of their cause, strengthen their resolution and confirm their loyalties, so that with dauntless hearts and dedicated wills they may work together for the coming of peace, and the glory of Thy Kingdom upon earth, through Jesus Christ Our Lord.

Amen

From the Chaplain of the Fleet.   Admiralty

This prayer was on a small piece of card intended to slip inside our cap.

Postscript

Alan came safely through the war and when next we met I found a tall, confident young man in place of the young seventeen year old brother I had last seen. Alan remained in the merchant navy travelling the seven seas.

Ken also came safely through the Italian campaign and back to Britain, although we never met again.

Gerry decided to stay in Australia and kept up a correspondence with Mother for a while.

The *Esperance Bay*, having survived all U-boats and storms, was finally sent to the breakers' yard in 1955.

All other friends of my service life I have lost track of, but would not be too surprised if some of them popped up suddenly some day. Life is full of surprises like that!

Postscript on 'Operation Market Garden'

A sequel to operation 'Market Garden' the Arnhem engagement, occurred a little more than one year later. My friend received a letter from the owner of the garden in Oostebeek which his troops had occupied for a time during the fighting. In his letter written in October 1945, five months after the end of hostilities, Mr Van Daalen described what had happened after my friend had left his garden.

He had acted as a guide to a British officer trying to reach part of the river where there was believed to be a steam-ferry. They were warned by others that there were a number of German snipers in the vicinity and were unable to get through. Heavy fighting continued throughout the area.

> 'When the firing became so heavy that only the cellar was comparatively safe we (himself, wife and small son) retired there. . . . The Germans kicked the front door open, searched the house, started pillaging and took a door to carry wounded away. We were very depressed for the taste of liberty had been very good. The next day they made a Red Cross station of our house and used all our linen, blankets

and mattresses. All was soaked with blood.'

'In the evening I went to the farmhouse to see if my neighbours were still alive.'

He describes the scene he found there as 'most horrible'. There were several dead or wounded allied soldiers lying unattended in the rooms and passages. The farmer's family he found in the cellars, unhurt, but very frightened. Van Daalen and the family did what they could for the wounded, giving them a drink and cigarette, bandaging some and providing blankets for the night. All this was done while the heavy shooting continued.

The following morning Van Daalen returned to the farmhouse and found the dead and wounded had been robbed by German soldiers and still had no medical attention. He tried to obtain help for them from the German medics, but was not very successful. The Germans seemed to be very short of medical orderlies or doctors. He discovered other Allied troops in a stable and in a cellar, but could do little for them. The heavy firing prevented any wounded, Allied or German, from being carried out of the area.

Van Daalen continues:

'Later in the day I was ordered out of the cellar by the SS and it was with some misgivings that I went upstairs. However, things were not so bad. It was a Dutch Nazi fighting with the SS who wanted to lay down arms and make good his escape. He asked for civilian dress. He told me that he belonged to the Herman Goering battalion (about 1,000 strong) and that after three days fighting only 105 survived. All officers were killed. He estimated that their losses were the heaviest of the whole war, mainly due to the fact that it was of boys from seventeen to nineteen years of age with only six weeks' practice. After one murderous assault their officers had to chase them back with their revolvers. I didn't want to give him a suit of mine, on the other hand I thought that every deserter was a danger less.'

Van Daalen advised the man to go to the farmhouse whose occupants had already left the area and find some clothes there. This the man did.

Van Daalen discovered from this deserter that the Allied soldiers he had seen in the stable and cellar had been taken prisoner. The Van Daalen family spent ten more days in what was left of their house, listening when they could to the wireless in their cellar under the very noses of the occupying Germans. All wireless was strictly forbidden by the Germans, so they took a great risk. They were waiting and hoping to hear of the arrival of Lt General Dempsey's forces.

'We reckoned he would come so we stayed, but when his heavy artillery started a barrage the ninth night, I thought the risk for my family too great, so we prepared to depart the next morning.'

However, they were unable to get away as the Poles had the road under their fire and fired at everything that moved there. An Allied doctor who came from the side of the Rhine controlled by the Polish troops asked Van Daalen to act as an interpreter for him in order to get medical help to wounded allied soldiers near the gasworks.

'The Germans were very sour about it and said it was only for spying. . . . The result I never heard.'

The barrage continued again that night.

'Everybody was very afraid, our cellar was packed with Germans. Conditions became quite unbearable. There was no water and only a little food. All was dirty and the whole house was shot up. When the farmhouse was fiercely burning we had to watch that our house didn't burn too, pulling all the

196

curtains from the windows. All the panes were gone of course. It was a horrible mess. The only person of the whole lot who was not afraid was my little son, who had only one care, that his dog, a fox terrier, shouldn't run away. And when doggie went for an urgent mission into the garden he insisted that the whole family should go out also and find him back. . . .'

The next morning they packed what they could on to their bicycles and left early and quickly to avoid the firing from the Polish positions. They went to Benneckorn, noticing some burnt-out German tanks on the way. After a few weeks there they were ordered to leave the area as the Germans made it *Spen-Gebiet*, a prohibited area for all Dutch people.

Val Daalen, a resistance member, made contact with a group and they were successful in returning 130 Allied Airborne troops to Allied lines on the other side of the Rhine. He continued with other members of the resistance in carrying out many dangerous missions to help the Allies' cause, until one unlucky day when they were rounded up by the Gestapo and sent to Woblin concentration camp in Mecklenburg.

'We had a very bad time. Nearly all our friends and comrades died. Only eleven out of a group of 300 came back. I came back on 10 May with typhus and my wife hardly recognised me. The Americans liberated us. The first time we were liberated on 17 September, we laughed, now we wept.'

He mentions many of his friends who died, some from starvation and dysentery, and his bitterness is very apparent. When he had recovered sufficiently, he and his family returned to Oosterbeek to try and repair the damage done.

'Yesterday we got electric light again, he says in his letter dated 16 October 1945. 'Our shop has opened for some time; business as usual. Life returns to normal. We are free – thank you – we won't forget. . . . You are always welcome in our home.'

These are only some extracts from a long letter, but they give us a picture of the dreadful hardships that were endured by all. At the beginning of his letter are these words:

'We are quite aware that some kind of history has been made in the last years and though a large part of our village is in ruins, we don't think the price too high for the final result: Liberty. Liberty is for us, who for five years were under the yoke of the Germans, the finest word in the world.'

The people of Arnhem have not forgotten and in this year of 1993, nearly fifty years after the event, they still hold a reunion and commemorative service to honour those who gave their lives in this venture.

The actual participants lessen as the years go by. Mr Van Daalen, the writer of the letter quoted, is no longer alive, but he and others are remembered by the people of the town and villages and by all the men who were involved in the drama of Operation 'Market Garden'.

AUTHOR'S CORRECTION

Page 26 Line 11
delete 'photograph'
Page 33 Line 5
should read 'were attended
by teams of RAF and WAAF
(Womens' Auxilary Air Force)
personnel.'
Page 41 Line 2
should read 'Oct.1939'